"Wherefore for the sake of fulfilling their lusts (women) consort even with devils."
-Heinrich Kramer, 1486 "Malleus Maleficarum" (The Hammer of Witches)

TESTIMONIALS

"Arla Dahl has delivered another superbly crafted, exhilaratingly erotic tale with the added bonus of a deliciously original historical setting. THE ACCUSED draws the reader into a roiling world torn between lethal paranoia and sexual combustion, dread and incapacitating pleasure, as tender flesh is ruthlessly tested for evidence of witchcraft. THE ACCUSED is historical erotica at its finest!

–best-selling author, Pam McKenna

"This story is perfect to curl up with on a spooky autumn night, with a cup of hot cider, and get lost in a decadent place where your wicked fantasies and fears come true."

–erotic romance author, Debra Druzy

"If you're expecting Ms. Dahl's second installment in this series to be more of the same, think again. Same night, same characters, same richly-detailed writing. But the story takes the reader on a completely different journey--just as explosively erotic as the first but with unexpected twists and surprises that keep the pages turning. But Reader Beware: Do yourself a favor and find a reading area with plenty of air-conditioning. This book is so hot a fan won't be of much help."

– 2013 RITA Finalist, Pamela Hearon

ACKNOWLEDGMENTS

Story creation brings thrilling moments of discovery as well as terrifying moments of self-doubt. Without the support of friends and family, the latter would devour the former, and so my deepest gratitude goes to all those who listened to my concerns as I moved forward with this project, pointed to the story's strengths when I saw only its flaws, and gave me room to find my own way through the fog before waving a guiding hand.

I can't thank you all enough.

Immoral Virtue Trilogy
Arla Dahl

Book Two
The Accused

"All witchcraft comes from carnal lust,
which is in women insatiable."
~Heinrich Kramer, 1486
"Malleus Maleficarum" (*The Hammer of Witches*)

DEDICATION

For the women who danced and smiled and teased,
being all they were meant to be,
at a time when doing so could result
in damnation and death.

FROM THE AUTHOR

Dear Reader,

The witch hysteria of the 1600s gripped the hearts and minds of many. During that time, a person could be accused of witchcraft for almost any behavior deemed questionable or improper. Dancing, bawdy speech, disagreements with neighbors whose crops soon wilt...

Once brought before the court, many would confess. They were all sinners, even the most pious, and they believed sinning permitted Satan into their heart. They would seek forgiveness, repent. The court would often show mercy, understanding this human weakness. It was mostly women who would confess, who would fall upon their knees, aching to be released from Satan's hold.

Men who stood accused were more likely to respond with righteous indignation. They were not so foolish or weak as to succumb to the teasing or temptations of Satan. How dare it be suggested they might.

A few women resisted as well. Those who did were subdued by friends, neighbors or, perhaps, as had happened, by random passersby called in by the court.

Imagine, strangers tearing at your clothes, ignoring your screams, snatching at you until you stood naked. Hands all over you. Prodding. Probing. Seeking the devil's mark. If you fought them, you must have much to hide.

If saving your life meant sacrificing your soul by lying, would you confess? Would you fight for your good name, and hope sanity would prevail?

Think before you answer, but do not think overlong for either option could be yet another trick of evil.

May you be unmarked.

Arla

The Accused

Arla Dahl

"...there was a defect
in the formation of the first woman,
since she was formed from a bent rib,
that is, a rib of the breast,
which is bent as it were
in a contrary direction to a man.
And since through this defect
she is an imperfect animal,
she always deceives."

~Heinrich Kramer, 1486

Chapter One

Wedick Colony, 1682
    – One hour past the Midnight Moonrise
A cold foul mist hovered in the moonlit air, like the gossamer veil of evil's deception. Waves of dread and savage lust snaked through the torch-bearing mob still clustered before the governor's manor. The crowd taunted five women bound on the grounds, but dared not step past the open gates, lest the devil be tempted to curse their souls.

Midnight had come and gone, and still they remained, eager for their governor's first decree. Anger soared high. Fear wedged deep. Yet their question lingered – be there witches among them?

Two men rushed forward, breaking free of the crowd.

One shouted at the accused. "Deceivers, all!"

"Strip them bare!" called the other, his torch held high. "Let us test them ourselves!"

The crowd pressed closer to the gate as their taunts grew louder, as their demands grew more urgent. Their torches bobbed and swayed as they moved, and pitch-tainted smoke swirled upward and sideways, writhing through the air like wayward sprites, surrounding the accused and accusers alike.

"Burn them lest they damn us all!"

This shrill cry rose above the rest, cutting through the din from the crowd, inciting others to call for the same, for only burning would rid their village of witches.

"Burn them! Burn them!"

The women they cursed stood silent, their bound limbs spread wide. Their slippers and petticoats were poor defense against the bitter night air. Their torn gaping shifts no defense against the crowd's biting stares. Torch smoke watered their eyes and burned their throats. It tempered their tears and cries as they bore the shame of being so crudely displayed.

The watchman, with his bare bulging arms crossed over his leather-clad chest, his face hooded so the devil might not see him, stood beside the women.

He took a wide and deliberate step toward the anxious mob. "There will be no talk from you of burning this night!" His voice was strong and firm. "That is for our governor to decide!"

A low grumble made its way through the crowd, and then a woman pointed to the accused bound last in the row. "Bring her to us now!"

Elizabeth Hobbs looked at the angry and frightened eyes of the crowd as all turned to her. She wished they would see her, their neighbor. Not a stranger. Not a witch.

She trembled against her restraints. Her wrists and ankles ached as the ropes binding them chafed her flesh, yet she would welcome that chafing over the crude filthy touch of the crowd. She lifted her gaze to the moon, high and bright in the heavens. If fear of being found marked had not silenced her prayers, she would offer a plea for the moon to move swiftly. To shorten the hours where light battled night, for if her innocence were proven, daylight would free her. But if the devil's mark were spied somewhere upon her body, then even daybreak would not lift the darkness.

The watchman turned to her, his blue eyes piercing from behind his black hood. His leather jerkin strained to cover the broad expanse of his chest beneath it, his breeches pulled snug against his hips and his thighs.

Every nerve within her convulsed as his heavy booted step brought him closer to her. If she could find her voice, she would beg for mercy. Instead, as the space between them dwindled, she lifted her chin. High, proud.

He stood before her then, so close they breathed the same air. She trembled, aware of him, of the crowd. Of her own helplessness.

An eternity passed with his gaze locked on hers. She expected it to be cold, hard. Accusing. Instead, she felt a warm flicker of compassion from him. Though perhaps that was merely her wish, her need to find sanity amongst the madness.

He lifted his hands to her torn shift and she drew a halting breath. Held it and waited. She shivered when his fingertips brushed the flesh between her breasts before closing over the tattered fabric there.

"They will see you now," he said. "The governor has so ordered."

Before she could voice a plea of reason, he ripped her shift further, spread it wide and exposed her breasts fully.

3

Cold wet air licked at her nipples, making her feel more naked than she had ever felt before. He had no right to bare her this way. She had not chosen this, to be bared and examined by the crowd. She, as the others bound beside her, would relinquish pride and submit to their governor only. To save their lives—nay, their souls—they would allow him to examine their flesh, inch by naked inch, to prove themselves pure and unmarked by the beast. Yet the crowd awaited. Eager to have their fill. Greedy in their fear-driven lust. She fought against her restraints, fought against the watchman, fought to find her voice as she thrashed about.

He gripped her bound wrists, pressed his body to hers. His hard chest crushed her breasts, pushed her back to the massive wooden X that held her firmly in place, stopping all movement, all struggle.

"Cease!" His harsh whispered word came out in a moist hiss that touched her cheek. "I built that which holds you. Do not think you can break free."

He eased back and though she trembled, she no longer struggled. "To what end would you fight?" he asked. "They will not let you pass the gate."

She looked at the crowd, still shouting, demanding she be cut loose and brought before them. She knew many of them. Had trusted them. Others, she had never seen before. She was evil to their fear- and rage-filled eyes. That rage turned her fear into something harder. Something she could barely control. Something they would deem powered by the beast himself – pride and a willful disdain.

"Fear makes them hunger," he said in nearly a whisper. "A morsel will slake their appetite until the governor's decree."

"They have no right..."

"If you are marked..."

"I am not."

"If you resist, they will believe you have much to hide and they will see you anyway."

From her struggles, her shift had fallen back into place. He smoothed his hand down along its edge, brushed it aside, exposed her again. "Do you wish to withdraw consent?"

She thought to say yes, for she had not consented to this. It was by the governor's order that she and the others be tested by all. Only then would they be permitted to enter the manor to be examined by him. To submit this way, he had said, was to release pride. To show all that the beast and his power had not captured their souls. She could not fight. To do so would mean she had been marked. To do so would mean her life.

"Nay." The word did not want to be heard. She spoke it again. "I do not withdraw consent."

"May you be unmarked," he said, soft as a prayer. He cupped his cold rough hands beneath her breasts. She gasped at the touch, but he did not let go. "You have seen what they will do." His voice was soft, almost tender. "The more you fight..." He lifted her breasts in his palms as though gauging the weight of her. "...the more pleasure it will give them to punish you." He brushed his thumbs down over the tops of them in a touch light as butterfly wings against her.

Tingles scurried over her flesh and she sucked in a breath, fought against the sensations.

In a bold and shameful gesture, he flicked his thumbs against her nipples, sending a bolt of shocking pleasure racing through her. She whimpered, alarmed by her body's instant betrayal.

She had heard the others cry when he touched them. From the tears they shed, she feared his touch would be cruel and punishing. Instead, it was gentle. Stirring. As he caressed her, understanding grew. It was not the pain but the shame that made them cry, for his touch did not wound but arouse.

He closed his fingers over her nipples in a soft grip she felt through to her core. Rousing her as it heated and throbbed. She wished it to stop, yet her body craved more. And the townsfolk witnessed it all.

Then he pinched, hard, piercing her nipples with pain as great as the flooding heat beneath her petticoat. Her cry came from low in her throat, a deep wounded and wanting sound that mingled with shouts from the crowd.

"It is good to cry out," he said, still pinching. "For only a witch cannot feel."

Her nipples throbbed in his grasp, her core still betrayed her. Then, without warning, he dropped his hands from her, letting her breasts fall with only his gaze to capture them.

He knelt before her then and freed her ankles. In that instant, she closed her eyes, unsure whether she had the courage to go on. Then he moved beside her and released the ties binding her wrists. She lowered her arms to her sides, noted how her hands trembled, but then he captured them in his and bound them behind her.

"You must be brave now, Elizabeth." He spoke so softly she wondered if he had whispered the same way to the others. "It is time." His hand, closing on her upper arm, was like the icy cold touch of death.

All she was screamed for her to resist, yet she moved with him as he drew her closer to the crowd. The thick wet air nearly suffocated her and she fought for each breath.

Her legs grew heavy, threatened to hold her back. Her step faltered, and his hand grew tighter on her arm.

"Do not grant them the pleasure they seek." He made her halt before him, facing the crowd.

They quieted, their gazes wide, their eagerness palpable. He released her and she stood there, her breasts heaving with every tremor of dread-filled anticipation.

Then he stood behind her and a flutter of fear rushed down her spine. Though she knew what was to come, she was not yet prepared. He gripped her shift from behind, his knuckles grazing her neck, a touch deceivingly gentle. Drawing mightily on courage, she steeled herself against overwhelming shame as he drew her torn shift from her shoulders. He eased it down her arms to her elbows, baring her fully to the waist.

A hushed murmur wafted through the crowd and she could do naught but stand shamed and defenseless before them. As was their wish. The watchman tugged the fabric at her elbows, held it tight, forced her arms back, her naked chest out.

He shoved her forward then, presenting her for inspection as he had presented the others. "Be this a witch?"

A roar came from the crowd and then greedy hands of all sizes and shades of filth reached through the gate. Touching her. Testing her. The crowd cheering as she labored to avoid their grasp.

It was no use. With each step she took beyond their reach, the watchman pushed her closer. He walked her slowly down the line of them, assuring each a part in this vulgar and punishing inspection.

Calloused fingers captured her nipples. Scraped against them. Pinched. Pulled. Delicate hands, rough hands, cupped her breasts. Squeezed, scratched. More hands reached for her. Cold hands all. They snatched and slapped at every bit of her exposed flesh. Taunts grew deafening, and a dizzying rumble of shame curled deep down to her soul. But she did not cry out, did not close her eyes. They had taken her freedom, taken her good name. They would not take her courage, too.

"Enough!" With mercy, the end of the line grew near and the watchman pulled her beyond the crowd's longest stretch. "Who would deny her breasts are pure?" No one spoke and he tugged her backward, farther away from the gate.

She gratefully let him take her to where the air was cooler, the roar of the crowd less deafening. Relieved to have passed this first examination.

She did not struggle as he bound her wrists to the X once more. She did not resist when he spread her legs wide and secured her ankles, nor when he tucked her shift in at her sides, assuring a clear view for the crowd of her now sore and sullied flesh.

Perhaps, the worst had passed.

She closed her eyes for a brief moment, comforting herself with the thought that, somehow, the rest of her examination would be less difficult, inside, with the governor.

There was movement from the manor. A hush fell around her as all eyes turned toward it.

Governor Jameson Foster stood tall and proud atop the stairs, regal in his quilted doublet and fitted breeches, while a naked Abigail Prescott stood brave and poised beside him. Her breasts bore the marks of severe testing. Her body glistened as though coated with oils. Her pubis was bare, all hair stripped from that most intimate part of her. The sight filled Elizabeth with dread, for she now feared the worst might be yet to come.

Governor Foster led Abigail down the stairs, his dark eyes skimming the crowd before resting on the women with Elizabeth – bound, bared and afraid. He turned back to the crowd with Abigail beside him. And then he called out, "Who will clothe this innocent woman?"

Shouts and cheers rang from the crowd as several women rushed forward, circling Abigail, touching her, layering her with clothing…

Elizabeth shared tearful smiles with those bound beside her, relieved to know the first among them to be examined had been found unmarked and innocent.

And then the watchman went to the frightened Rebecca, bound at the opposite end. Hardly twenty, fair of complexion and hair, she trembled. Seeming not to notice her terror, he cut her restraints and passed her into the governor's charge. The governor wrapped his large hands around her breasts, squeezing them, caressing them, weighing them. Inspecting them much as the watchman and the crowd had done before. He led her to the gate, and Elizabeth feared he would make Rebecca walk the line yet again. Instead, he beckoned Abigail, now properly dressed and standing with the crowd. She went to him, the top of her head barely reaching his shoulder. He spoke to her but she did not reply and he waited. Silent. Seeming to grow impatient. And then Abigail lifted her hands, slowly, hesitantly, and touched the girl's breasts.

The girl trembled but did not resist as Abigail's fingers sunk into her white flesh, kneading her, caressing her, pinching her with a sudden eagerness Elizabeth did not understand. Abigail murmured something, and the governor nodded, his dark expression softening with a near tender approval.

Elizabeth trembled with concern. What had he done to Abigail within the manor? Had he stirred her with touches as soft as the watchman's? Elizabeth fought a new shudder of fear. Could she permit the governor to do the same to her? To see her completely bare? To touch her? Shave her? Fill her with desire she should not feel?

No. She could not. She would resist. She would deny all budding sensations...

But it is only a witch who does not feel...

As if hearing her thoughts, the governor turned slowly, looking to where she stood bound, and settled his gaze firmly upon hers.

His eyes were unlike those of the watchman. They held no tenderness. No compassion. Only suspicion. And authority. She bowed her head, breaking the contact, then closed her eyes, aware his unyielding gaze still lingered upon her. The strength of it heated her body in ways it should not, and though she tried to discourage all thoughts of submitting to his examination, she knew, to prove her innocence, there would be no other way.

She looked at the angry, shouting mob. They would not be convinced. No plea for reason, no baring nor submission, would be enough to quell their fears and sinful lust. Nay. Only a decree from their beloved governor would do.

Chapter Two

Abigail feared for the others, fully aware what lay ahead for them.

Her governor turned toward the manor, forcing Rebecca to lead the way, much as he had forced Abigail an hour past.

And now, Abigail followed, her step less sure than his. She had offered her assistance, and he had accepted, for daybreak would not wait and five more were to be examined this night.

She spared a glance at the other women, still bound, their shifts torn and gaping to the waist, leaving them open to the cold and to the crowd. The matron, with her eyes closed, seemed to pray, while some beyond the gate cried that her words were meant to conjure the devil.

The sisters – twins they were – exchanged encouraging glances, one less certain than the other.

Elizabeth, bound last in the row, with hair the color of a setting sun, remained alert and defiant. She had focused her gaze shamelessly, insolently, on their governor a moment prior, and now set it upon the crowd, searing through them as though loathing, not fear, had gripped her.

Abigail understood. She had felt that same defiance, but none of the accused would escape their fate. The governor's examination would be as shameful and grueling for each of them as it had been for her. Worse if he discovered The Mark upon their bodies.

He neared the manor with Rebecca and Abigail hastened her step to reach them. "Good Sir?"

He did not stop to hear her words.

She lifted her skirts to her ankles and climbed the wooden stairs beside him, hurrying to match his stride. "The women…" she said. "The rest…perhaps you will permit them to come inside? Together?"

Without reply, Jameson pulled the manor doors open and ushered Rebecca inside.

Abigail glanced back at the bound women. She would find a way to make these examinations easier. For them. For Jameson. And for herself.

She turned away and stood poised to enter the manor. A slithering chill of dread stopped her one step before the threshold, for a mere hour past she had been as Rebecca, bared and bound, with Jameson's hand at her back, permitting her not to dally, not to think beyond that moment, not to note her surroundings nor question her fate. But she had chosen to submit to his examination, the same as she now chose to assist with the others.

She dropped her skirts and entered the manor. The massive front hall loomed before her. Candles, lining the walls, shuddered in the cold breeze from the open doors, their flames sending shadows thrashing over the broad-planked floor and wide stairway. Beyond the dim entry lay a cavernous hole of blackness she had not noticed before. What rooms stood within that gaping void, she did not know, nor did she hope to learn.

Nary a hint of what happened to the accused within the manor had ever escaped it. Nor would it. Trapped within were tears of shame, cries of horror and pitiful sighs of inescapable pleasure. Pleasure Jameson could grant. Or withhold.

Abigail closed the doors behind her, locking the cold air and raucous crowd outside. Only the thud of Jameson's booted step and brush of Rebecca's slippers remained within the imposing space.

Abigail hurried after them, down the hall and into Jameson's antechamber. She pushed the heavy chamber door until its iron latch fell into place with a sharp peremptory clank.

Rebecca whimpered as Jameson led her toward the hearth. Abigail ached to comfort her but she could not, for Rebecca's fear and shame would not soon be assuaged.

"Why are you here, Rebecca?" The low timbre of Jameson's voice, though gentle, held no hint of comfort.

"It has been said I am a witch," she said with more strength than Abigail anticipated, "but I am not, for I did but dance."

Jameson studied the girl's eyes as he stood inches before her, touching her with no more than his gaze. Abigail's pulse quickened as though it was she who stood beneath his scrutiny.

Doubt assailed her in that instant. Could she stand witness, could she aid him as he examined, as he touched and aroused, another? When he had touched her, when she knew not what he expected and was frightened, as Rebecca surely was now, it was only his practiced and patient hand that had broken her resistance. His every touch had made her feel great shame, immense heat and ultimate release.

"Abigail."

Startled, she gasped and looked up at him, certain from his hard stare that he knew where her thoughts had gone. "Good Sir?"

"Gather the oils and set them upon the table."

She hurried to comply, and crossed the room to the huge chest where all manner of testing instruments lay, many crude and cruel. She lifted the heavy lid and the hinges creaked in a low aching moan of surrender. Much as she had before. Much as Rebecca soon would. Lest she be marked.

The amber vials of oil lay nestled within, fragile and innocuous beside angry contraptions forged to cause great harm – irons, clamps, claws and more. But this night, beneath Jameson's practiced touch, the accused would have naught to fear. Unlike governors before, who wrenched confessions through pain, Jameson sought to prove innocence through pleasure.

She lifted the vials. The woodsy scent of one oil still lingered upon her flesh. The richness of the other still coated her most intimately. She closed her eyes. All but felt Jameson's fingers probing her, his oiled hands slick against her naked flesh, touching her as no man had ever touched her before...

"I will see your eyes, Rebecca." He used a different voice with the girl now. A softer tone, stern yet calm. "Do not look away."

They stood silhouetted, as though lovers, face to face before the glowing hearth. Jameson's broad body towered over Rebecca's, his finger beneath her chin, tilting her face toward his.

"If you are marked... anywhere," he said in a whisper, "I will know."

He trailed a finger from Rebecca's chin down to her neck and over the ridge of her shoulder, a single stroke, slow and steady. The caress pebbled Rebecca's flesh as he traced back to brush the slight swell of her breast. Painting her with his touch the same as he had painted Abigail's. And Abigail breathed with them. Slowly. Deeply. The tingle of Jameson's touch, the heat it had created deep within her, as vivid for her now as before.

"You cannot hide," he said in a tone so tender, the words seemed not to matter.

He shifted his hand and whispered the back of it downward, over the top of Rebecca's breast. The girl swayed and seemed to tremble. His touch did not falter. The movement slight. Deliberate. The sight magnificent. Haunting. As though flames of lust had leapt from the hearth, rousing them all with a heat of a different kind.

"Do you understand?" He brushed his hand lower, then flicked a knuckle against her nipple.

The girl jolted and hissed in a breath as sudden as Abigail's.

Jameson turned then, his gaze falling upon Abigail in a caress so bold, so heated, she felt bared before him once again. He had uncovered the secrets of her body, stirred them even now, and told her with merely this glance how well he knew her desires.

With great effort, she met his gaze, held it.

"You dawdle, Abigail," he said, his tone unforgiving.

She offered a slight bow of her head, wishing not to rouse his anger, for sweet Rebecca would bear the burden. And then she brought the vials to the table, setting them on the wide surface where, an hour past, she had obeyed his commands and laid back. Daring not to resist as he bound her there, spread and bare. Opened to his gaze and his touch. The iron rings mounted at the corners now lay empty, the leather straps that had secured her, nowhere to be found. Would he bind Rebecca there as well? And the others?

Abigail turned to see Jameson stroll the room, leaving Rebecca alone by the hearth. Unhurried in step and motion, he took withered candles from their sticks and replaced them with new. Lighting them. One by one.

And Rebecca waited. Exposed. Bound. Her back to him. Knowing not what fate awaited her. It had been the same for Abigail. And her fear had weakened her. Surely Jameson knew.

He was masterful. Priming his charges before he examined them. Making them most malleable without so much as a touch, assuring when he chose to touch, they would think only of the need he stirred within them.

Her own body warmed now as when he had tested her. As when he had coated her body in the oils, heating her not merely where he touched but deeper, stirring her with shameful pleasures she could not deny, his knowing hands as gentle as they were demanding.

It would be so for Rebecca as well.

Abigail wished to embrace the girl. As much to soothe her as to block her lovely body from Jameson's view, but she could not. To prove Rebecca's innocence, no part of her body would remain unseen, untouched. Unquenched. It would be shameful, but she would respond, willingly. For if the secrets of her flesh were not revealed, Jameson would deem her marked, touched by the beast. Deadened to pleasure. Or worse, deadened to pain.

Abigail stirred. Unsure how to ease her own restlessness. Aware as she was of her own rising tensions, for she would endure it all again. No longer as an accused, but as witness. And accomplice.

Jameson met her gaze through a mirror on the far wall. "Set the kettle to heat, Abigail."

Before she could respond, he went to Rebecca, stood before her and held a candle high between them. Rebecca's gaze did not stay on his as he commanded but fell to the floor. Yet he said nothing of it. Instead, he turned, the warning spark in his eyes striking Abigail fully, and she dared not ignore it.

She hoisted the heavy kettle from the floor and brought it to the hearth, quickly hanging it above the flame.

"You have no reply, Rebecca?" He brushed the girl's hair from her face in a slow tender gesture, fondling a strand that fell upon her shoulder before he laid it at her back. "You cannot hide. Do you understand?"

Rebecca lifted her gaze, whether in silent surrender or supplication, Abigail did not know.

"Unless..." He coiled his hand through Rebecca's hair, held it taut, tugged until her head tipped back. "...you would, instead, be judged by those who linger beyond the gates."

Abigail recoiled at the thought of Rebecca at the mercy of the crowd.

Rebecca jolted as though struck. "Nay." She uttered the word with force and fear. Her breaths ragged, her head tipping further back. "I...would not. Their touch... It is cruel."

Jameson released her hair and closed his eyes briefly, seeming to share Abigail's relief.

"Then you freely choose your fate this hour?"

"Aye."

With his fingertips, he caressed the girl's cheek, her neck, his thumb sweeping over the hollow at her throat. "For what purpose do you choose this fate?"

"To prove I am not a witch."

"That is good." He stepped closer to her, stopping only when his linen doublet was pressed to her breasts. "Tell me, Rebecca..." His voice came from low in his chest, low and alluring, "for whom did you dance that night?"

"I danced for no one."

He cupped his hands to her shoulders, brushed them over her arms. His gaze, his touch, searching her flesh for the devil's mark as he had searched Abigail's. "No one?"

Rebecca shivered beneath his caress, her eyes seeming heavy, her breaths unsteady even as she gazed up at him. "No one, save myself."

He tipped his head closer, as though he might share a kiss, and Rebecca's gaze dropped to his lips, her own parting.

Abigail felt as an intruder. Inexplicably pained by the intimate sight of them.

"I wish to know…" His voice was a whisper. True in its sincerity, false in its tenderness. "…is it often you dance alone?"

"Nay, I did but once."

He merely looked at her, said not a word. Then he shook his head slowly and Abigail held her breath.

"I fear you speak untruths, Rebecca," he said.

She gasped and he circled her, stopping when he stood at her back.

"I will hear truth from your lips." His arm came around her. "By your choice…" His hand flattened at the waist of her petticoats, then grazed up over her torn shift, over her bare breasts, her neck. "…or by my command." His fingers circled the pale column of her throat, stroked it slowly. "I ask again, Rebecca." He tipped her head back, forcing her to look up at him as he looked down from behind. "How many times have you danced… alone?" His tone had changed. Impatience edged it deeper. His fingers no longer stroked her neck, but circled it, gripped it.

Abigail feared his intent. "Good Sir?"

He spared her the briefest glance, warning her. Silencing her. Then he turned his gaze back to Rebecca, stroked her neck once more.

The girl trembled, gulped in air, then stared, frightened, her silent mouth open as he gripped her neck again.

Abigail's body still bore the marks of his harsh unyielding touches. She had feared them, had feared her responses to them. Yet it was a response he required then, as now. But Rebecca did not know… "Good Sir."

"As you value the air you breathe," he said to Rebecca, "I value truth." He tipped Rebecca's head back further. Whispered. "You will speak it now." He loosened his hold, stroked her neck once more.

"I have danced many times," she said, and her tears fell. "When I might glimpse my shadow."

"Your shadow? Or the beast?"

"Nay! Not the beast! Fire in the hearth set my own shadow upon the wall. It moved as I moved. 'Twas but a dance."

Jameson turned her to face him. "You must know…" he said, "…to dance so, is to rouse the beast."

She cried openly and it was a pitiful sound.

Gently, he dried her tears as they fell. Shook his head and leaned in closer to her, his parted lips a mere breath from her ear. "Dance for me." He smoothed his hands over her face, her neck. Her shoulders. His touch light. His voice hushed.

Rebecca trembled and Abigail sighed. Relived. Roused.

"Dance as you danced that night." He skimmed his fingertips lower, the move so slow, so gentle Abigail's own skin rippled. He released the ropes binding Rebecca, and tossed them to the floor. "Show me," he said, and led Rebecca from the hearth until she stood in the middle of the room. There, firelight writhed at her back, setting her shadow on the far wall. Her naked hips and thighs visible through her petticoats, her arms unbound, her shift still low and baring her breasts. "Prove to me you danced not for Satan's pleasure," Jameson said, "but for your own."

He stepped back, but Rebecca did not move. Abigail went to her, stood behind the girl, knowing well how Rebecca had danced, for the hours they had spent bound with the other women had borne truths from each. Truths humble to horrid. Rebecca's dance had brought terror to her mistress' heart, while the twin's ardor drained men of their abilities. And the others, their imagined crimes such that a sane man would see no harm.

"You must," she said then clasped Rebecca's hands, held them high, extending the girl's arms out to her sides. "Was it not so?" She lifted Rebecca's hands higher, over the girl's head, allowing her shift to fall back into place. "Do what you must." She smoothed her own hands down the length of Rebecca's arms. "Prove your innocence." And then she circled her, and took a step back toward Jameson.

Only Rebecca's arms moved, drifting downward, slowly, like leaves in an early autumn breeze. And then she turned and her scent, light and clingy, wafted over them, changing the air the same as musk from cool dampened earth.

Abigail dared a glance at Jameson. His gaze did not leave Rebecca, but floated over her body. Her eyes, her hair, her flowing arms. The glimpse of bare breast, a tease in the firelight. Her thighs, her softly rounded hips, tender flesh caressed by the sheer fabric of her petticoats... the sight consumed Abigail as well. But Rebecca seemed unaware of her stunning form. She lowered her eyes demurely and twirled, a small smile, fleeting and free, grazed her lips. And then she lifted her gaze and Abigail turned to see where the girl looked.

Her shadow adorned the far wall. It loomed over them, as a man might loom over a woman. Swaying. Drifting. The same as Rebecca. It seemed the two danced together. Playfully. Innocently. With nary a hint of the malice for which she had been charged.

Jameson looked where they looked and Abigail took that moment to free the girl from her dance lest her rising pleasure bring concern to Jameson. "Good Sir, 'twas for her own pleasure," she said. "Surely that is clear."

"Aye," he said. "Yet pleasure so consumed is a knock upon Satan's door."

"And what of the pleasures consumed within these walls. Are they not a knock as well?"

"You forget your place, Abigail." His hard gaze lingered on hers and she dared not respond lest his anger rise then fall upon Rebecca. He turned for the chest and Abigail muffled a gasp, aware what he sought from within. And then he faced them again, a crop held tight in his fist.

He went to the wide table and leaned back on its edge. "Come here," he said, his gaze steady on Rebecca.

The girl's slippers swept the floor as she went to him, each step less sure than the one before.

"I do not believe your dance to be for Satan's pleasure," he said. "Yet Satan's pleasure takes many forms. I will know now if he has tasted yours. Disrobe."

The girl did not move, and Jameson made to rise, the calm patient tone of his voice contrasting with the intensity of his gaze.

Abigail hurried to Rebecca's side, gently taking the girl's hand in her own. "I know this to be difficult," she said, "for I have stood in your place."

She gently brushed a coil of Rebecca's lush yellow hair from her neck. "But you must not delay for others await." All of the accused would be judged by daybreak, whether by Jameson's decree or by voice of the crowd. The notion sent a cold shiver through Abigail. "Do what is asked." She looked at Jameson, gauging his temper, noting how his gaze lingered on her hand against Rebecca's bare shoulder. "And you shall soon be clothed again."

Rebecca trembled beneath Abigail's hand and held her torn shift closed at her breast. "I...cannot."

Abigail set herself between Rebecca and Jameson, her back to him. "Perhaps, if you vow to obey him this hour," she said, "he will permit you to turn your back whilst you disrobe." She dared a glance at him, certain there would be no harm in honoring this small request.

His nod was slow in coming, but when it did, Abigail turned Rebecca's back to Jameson and locked her own gaze on his over the girls' shoulder. Slowly, carefully, she peeled the shift from Rebecca's arms until it hung over her petticoat, baring Rebecca to the waist. The girl made to cover her breasts with her hands.

"You must not." Abigail grasped the girl's wrists, lowering her arms. "It is only the witch who hides what she has," she said, using the same words Jameson had used to encourage her. She smoothed her palm down the length of Rebecca's arm, as Jameson's gaze followed the path of her touch.

Abigail circled Rebecca then, a lithe figure, quivering in body and breaths, stopping when she stood at the girl's back. She lifted her gaze to a mirror on the far wall. Jameson looked back at her through it. Studying her, his gaze steady on hers as if she were still the object of this examination.

"Be there a mark upon her neck?" he asked.

Abigail brushed Rebecca's hair to the side and grazed her fingers gently over the back of Rebecca's neck. The girl tensed at the touch and Abigail let her fingers stray lower, slowly, gently brushing the line of her spine, remembering well the tingling warmth that had spread through her when Jameson touched her so. She smoothed her fingers to the sides, feeling only softness and warmth. Seeing only dimpled flesh. "I see no mark upon her neck, Good Sir. And neither upon her back."

"Her breasts, Abigail. Be they marked?"

Abigail hesitated. Her gaze on his through the mirror. His steady, insistent. She reached forward, gently sliding her fingertips along the soft swell of Rebecca's small breasts. Jameson's gaze lowered to her hands, the heat within his eyes encouraging her to continue. And Abigail cupped Rebecca's breasts in her palms, kneaded them, awed by their weight and tender plushness.

She allowed herself a small smile as Jameson's gaze slid from one breast to the other, aware it was her touches that attracted him. A ripple of pride swelled through her at having placed herself between him and this soft lovely creature.

When he drew his own unsteady breath, she eased her hands forward and captured Rebecca's nipples tightly between her fingers. Rebecca started, her whole body tensing as a small cry cut through her.

Abigail's own body felt alive, alert, for she felt the pleasure not just through her fingertips but to her core. Heat. Moisture. Longing. Her own breasts ached, her nipples hardened beneath her shift. Her body awakened now as when Jameson caressed her.

She looked at him, somehow knowing his gaze would still be upon her. It was steady, dark, as if desire filled him as well.

Flattening her palms to the small hard tips, she rubbed gently, touching Rebecca as she had never touched another. The softness of breasts was not unfamiliar to her, but rather the way they warmed beneath her hands, they way they seemed to swell with each sigh through Rebecca's lips.

Rebecca shuddered, falling back against Abigail as though the girl's legs were made liquid. The heat of Rebecca's body against hers stirred Abigail further. She thought of Jameson, pressed against her, lying atop her after he had permitted their release.

With a small smile teasing her lips, she dropped her hands from the girl's tender flesh. Resisted the urge to cup her own breasts as heat unfurled yet deeper within her.

Slowly, she lifted her gaze to Jameson's through the mirror. He did not blink. Did not speak. Did not reach out to her. Yet she ached. Felt warmed as though his strong hands were upon her again.

"Good Sir," she said, surprised by the breathless tone of her voice. "She felt my touch."

With a step achingly slow and sure, he circled them. Stopped only when he stood before them, the crop firmly in his grasp, a dark determination in his eyes as they searched Abigail's. "Yet it is your arousal which scents this space," he said.

She gasped and the smallest smile curved his lips. His gaze did not falter but held hers and she felt bare once more. Opened to him, her body responding to his eyes as to his touch.

His small smile faded. "Do not confuse the pleasure you feel with the pleasure you give," he said, then looked at Rebecca. "Fear-filled arousal is but an empty illusion." He touched his fingertips to Rebecca's lips, drew them down to her neck. "True passion…is oft hidden…" He flattened his palm between her breasts until her breathing grew shallow and quick. "…yet it can be coaxed from the innocent." He dropped his hand from Rebecca then raised the crop and touched the tip of it to her throat. "Though it can never be coaxed from the witch." He drew the stiff leather tip down the space between the girl's breasts then brushed it beneath the curve of one, slowly around its side, then along the top of it.

Though it was not her flesh beneath the crop now, Abigail remembered the coolness of the leather, the way her body shivered beneath its caress. She cupped Rebecca's breasts, lifted them and kneaded, as though they were her own.

Jameson lifted the crop, then gently swished it in wide strokes over Rebecca's nipples. Slowly, not stopping, back and forth, brushing them with the tip of the crop. Rebecca's body trembled against Abigail's, her breaths coming harder, filling her chest, lifting her breasts as though she sought more from the crop.

Then he pulled it away for the briefest moment, enough for Rebecca to draw a full breath before he snapped the tip of the crop to her nipple, once, twice, three times, not stopping.

Teasing the girl, ignoring her gasps and startled shivers, awakening her until a speckled flush colored her flesh. He turned his attention to the other nipple. Tapping it the same, making the tiny bud stand taller. The rhythm of his gentle strikes even. Persistent.

Rebecca's moans turned to whimpers, and her head lagged heavily against Abigail's shoulder, turning side to side as the stinging strikes Abigail well recalled continued. And Abigail held her, wrapped her arms around the girl's slender waist. Sighing with her. Encouraging her to feel each strike, respond to them...

Then Jameson drew his arm back and Abigail shuddered, well aware that the pain of his full force behind the crop would be unlike the teasing, torturous pleasure of his light swatting.

"Good Sir," she whispered, stopping him. "Must it be that way?"

She lightly brushed her fingertips over Rebecca's breasts once again and his gaze settled on her hands.

"Her flesh is most tender," Abigail said to him. "Even to the slightest touch."

Slowly, deliberately, she fanned her fingertips, one by one, over the hard little nipples there. She sighed as Rebecca quivered, then captured those aroused and sensitive tips between her fingers, lightly pressing them, twisting them. Steadying the girl as she whimpered, smiling softly as the rise and fall of Jameson's chest grew swift. Uneven. He, too, was aware of the sensations.

"A mere graze of your fingers will arouse her," she said. "Surely, flesh this tender, this responsive, is unmarked."

She cupped Rebecca's breasts in her palms, lifted them, held them out to him in offering.

"Touch her, Good Sir, as I have. Touch her, so you might see for yourself."

His gaze lingered on the girl's breasts as he stood unmoving. And then he looked into Abigail's eyes in a glance she sought, hot, steady. Demanding.

Without breaking the contact, he eased the crop's stout handle into a pouch at his hip then reached for Rebecca. His large hot hands covered her breasts from the top, kneading, as Abigail did from below. His gaze slowly lowering to their hands caressing Rebecca, meeting, circling the tender flesh completely, heating it, heating her and themselves.

"It is only the witch who cannot feel," he said, his voice coming from low in his chest.

"Rebecca..." Abigail smoothed her heated hands down to the girl's small waist. She circled them over Rebecca's quivering belly, then wrapped her arms around her, holding Rebecca back against her own body, enjoying the girl's softness and warmth. "Do you feel our touch?"

"Aye." It was a breath not a word, a breath hot as though heated, like the kettle upon the hearth.

Aware Rebecca was to be awakened further, Abigail lowered a hand to the bow at the girl's petticoats. "You will feel more..." she said and eased the bow loose. "We will see all of you now, touch all of you..."

A small shudder rippled through Rebecca. A small moan as well. She tensed, no longer languidly resting against Abigail.

"Hush," Jameson said in a tone so tender, even Abigail breathed a sigh. "Is this not why you are here?" He looked at Rebecca, as though only she stood before him.

"'Tis."

Abigail knew well the girl's reply did not match her thoughts, but could do naught, not now when proof of her innocence lay a few short moments away.

"Good Sir?"

At Jameson's nod, Abigail eased her hand beneath the loosened band at Rebecca's waist, then pressed her palm flat to the soft hot belly there. Her fingertips tangled within the mat of hair hidden beneath, raking through it gently.

"He will be thorough," she said, wishing to share all that would happen. But the accused must stand unaware. Their bodies awakened. Their need heightened. Their desires mercifully fulfilled by Jameson should he deem them unmarked. "Know all that happens here is to prove innocence." It was all she could say, for if the accused failed to respond – whether bewitched or forewarned – they would have no defense for their lives or their souls.

Rebecca gave a stilted nod and Abigail eased the petticoat over the slight swell of the girl's hips, letting it and the shift fall to the floor until she stood bare between them.

Abigail took strength from Jameson's gaze on her hands and smoothed them lower, over the girl's silken thighs then up again over her hips, her waist. Hoping to warm her, soothe her. Prepare her.

"You will come with me." She took Rebecca's hand in hers, helped her step from the pooled fabric at her feet and led her to the table, pleased she could be there to ease that which would occur next.

Abigail sat upon the table's edge then lifted the larger vial, filled with a thick unscented oil. She held it out to Jameson.

Shame surrounded this part of the examination, for it was crude and unnatural. Yet Jameson had prepared her for it. Patiently, purposefully. And her body had responded.

Rebecca would respond as well, for if she did not…

Jameson took the vial from Abigail then pressed his large hand to Rebecca's back, urging her to lean forward.

"Come," Abigail said to Rebecca. "Lay your head upon my skirts."

Rebecca hesitated and Abigail reached for her, pulled her closer, lower.

With a small cry of resistant awareness, Rebecca did as asked, bending at the waist and burying her face in Abigail's lap where Abigail held her.

"Hold fast unto me," she said, easing the girl's arms around her waist. "Do not let go." She brushed Rebecca's hair to the side, baring her back, and poured a few drops of the fragrant oil into her palm. Gently, in light fluid motions, she circled her hands over Rebecca from the girl's shoulders to the swell of her rump. "Her skin is most smooth," she said, looking at Jameson. "There is not a teat which I can see."

"Witches are most often marked in a spot dark and secret." He poured a few drops of the thick oil onto the table. "We must be diligent in our search." He set a hand low on Rebecca's back and used his booted foot to nudge her feet further apart.

Abigail knew not which was worse, having been as Rebecca was now, unaware of what to expect, or knowing the truth. And the shameful pleasure.

He looked at her and she could not look away. Even as he dipped his long thick pinkie into the oil and coated it until it glistened, she watched him. And then he turned to Rebecca and pressed a hand to her lower back.

"Widen your stance further," he said, to the girl, "and hold tight to Abigail."

Chapter Three

Abigail's assistance should have been of benefit to Jameson, but it was a hindrance. Her hands, small and pale, against the paler flesh of Rebecca, distracted him from his duties. Much like Abigail herself distracted him when she'd stood as Rebecca stood now.

He leaned across Rebecca. His thigh pressed to her slight hip as she stood bent, with her head in Abigail's lap. He cupped his hand to Rebecca's bare rump, smoothed over it, warmed it. Then he gave it a tight squeeze, welcoming her sharp gasp. The flesh beneath his palm paled further before it grew pink, responding to his touch as it should. She had not yet answered to pain. Only to the mild discomfort of the crop. Yet Abigail had been right. With the slightest touch, the girl's arousal scented the room, made her unsteady on her own feet.

He glanced at Abigail. She sat straight with her legs loose over the table's edge, her head tipped back and her eyes lowered, steady on his. Deep breaths whispered through her parted lips, lips he had sipped and still craved.

With her flattened hands, she drew circles over the girl's back, the earthy oil she spread there no match for the pungent scent of need spreading within these walls.

Rebecca's scent was light, almost as shy as she. Abigail's was meant to be known. It teased his senses, was as unexpected to him as it seemed to her, awakened as she had been to the beauty of breasts and silken flesh not her own.

It tormented him now. She tormented him. Whether purposely or from the newness of her arousal, he did not know, had not anticipated. He was to prove innocence. Not be seduced once again by Abigail's bewitching charms.

Abigail's circling hands reached lower, and her delicate fingertips grazed his wrist. The light innocent touch tingled through him like a thousand pins, teasing, testing his responses, his loins too eager in their reply. He cut his gaze, unwilling to be captivated by her again this night.

Rebecca had sworn innocence. He would do all to prove it so. Even subdue his own need yet again.

He dipped his pinkie in the oil once more, wishing not to harm the girl while needing to test her most secret spots. The beast, after sending his conquests into the throes of lust, would leave his black mark in a place hidden to all but those with the most discerning eye.

He shifted the hand already against the girl. Flattened his palm over her rump, then slid two fingers lengthwise into the deep crevasse between her tender cheeks. She tensed as an innocent would, but he would not be dissuaded. She was meant to feel this, to respond. To prove no hidden part of her, none shielded nor sensitive, had been deadened by the devil's touch.

He edged his fingers lower. Let the tips of them brush the cockled edge of her tight little passage. With a small moan, she shifted her hips but with Abigail's knees beneath her and his hand above, she had little place to go.

"Hush," he said, knowing this part was difficult for most, not only for the newness of it, not only for the fear, but for the pleasure it was sure to stir. Using only his fingertips, he spread her cheeks wide, exposing the tightness residing between them. She whimpered. Tensed further.

With his free hand slightly cupped, he smacked the underside of her fleshy cheek. She cried out as anticipated, from shock though not pain, for the strike was not hard. Still she tensed. He flattened his hand, landed another swat on the same spot. And then a third. Fourth. Fifth. Light enough to distract her. Hard enough to tinge her skin a deeper shade of pink, proving it was not deadened.

Her breaths came in quick little whimpers and he continued the strikes, still held her spread. Made her flesh yet more sensitive, her scent more apparent. Her body responding as he hoped. His own hand heating.

"You will draw a slow breath now, Rebecca." He smoothed his hand to the battered spot. "Long and slow," he said and glanced at Abigail. Her lips were further parted. Inviting. Her breaths so slow, so full they lifted her chest. Though her dress concealed the flesh there, he thought how she had been earlier, naked, presenting herself to his examination. Eager and open. Responsive. He looked down at his hand against Rebecca, cupping her cheek the way he would cup Abigail's breast if it were exposed to him again.

Tension eased from Rebecca as she breathed.

"Good," he said softly, then spread her wider with his fingers. "Another breath..."

As she calmed, he brushed his oiled finger over the tight little hole there. Short wispy caresses, up and down. Up and down. He did not stop, even as her tension returned. It was tension not meant as much to shut him out as to show proof of her mounting need.

"Easy. Deeply." He caressed her with slightly more force, watched Abigail as he did, unable to resist, eager to see her responses. She sat stiffly, her back bowed, her chest lifted, as though it were she, not Rebecca, beneath his hand.

He pressed his finger more firmly against Rebecca, softening the tightness there despite her resistance. "Breathe slow," he said but her every breath quivered as she drew it.

"She is frightened." Abigail's voice was like that of a lover. Breathy and faint. Tempting him to draw closer so he might hear it, feel it against his cheek.

Her fingers splayed wide across Rebecca's back, then clawed as she gently scraped the girl's flesh with her fingernails, making Rebecca tremble yet more.

"She appears most pure," he said. His wish was to be gentle, but there could still be a spot, yet unseen, that lay numb upon her body. All of her would be tested. "Close your eyes, Rebecca, and feel what I do."

She remained tight, stiff. Her tiny whimpers growing silent. And he increased pressure against her until he felt her muscles begin to relent, to open to him, allowing the very tip of his finger to slip inside of her.

"Perhaps..." Abigail's hot fingers closed around his wrist, the move dislodging him from the girl. "...it would be less difficult if she were tested elsewhere as well."

He searched Abigail's eyes. "I will hear your thoughts."

"'Tis her arousal in the air now." She inhaled deeply and gave him a small fleeting smile. "Touch her, Good Sir. Stir her further and perhaps this test will become more effective and... agreeable."

Her words, their meaning, were like a solid fist clamped around his cock. Building pressure swiftly as if that fist were oiled, resolute. Abigail's smile slowly returned, her gaze unwavering.

He understood her game, though perhaps, she did not. She was there to aid in these examinations so they might test all of the accused by dawn. Yet she tested him.

He straightened, taking Rebecca with him, his arm wrapped tight around her breasts, holding her back firmly to his chest. His gaze never left Abigail's, even as his free hand smoothed gently over Rebecca's soft belly.

"You will stand wide, Rebecca," he said, inching his hand lower until his fingertips skimmed her soft nether curls. He let them linger there, lightly thrumming as Abigail's gaze dropped to them. And then he slid his palm lower. Pressed it to Rebecca's inner thigh, forcing her legs further apart.

"Lift your skirts, Abigail," he said as his blood surged through him. "Know your pleasure so you might find hers."

Her eyes widened. Whether in hunger or shock, he did not know.

"Good Sir?" Her breathless tone exposed her need, her desire to do as he bid.

He pressed his hand more firmly to Rebecca's thigh, pushing her more solidly against him, the soft cushion of her bare rump a salve against his bulging cock. His need nearly bursting from him.

He held her there, unmoving, and forced his voice low and calm. "You would pleasure her, would you not?" he said to Abigail, certain she had not intended to do her own bidding. "To make this moment more agreeable?"

She hesitated, her bravery slipping, and he permitted himself a small smile. Sure her intent had been to arouse him while unaware his intent could be the same.

"Others await, Abigail." His voice was as tight, as thick, as his cock. "Yet you dawdle."

She eased off the table, her gaze shifting to Rebecca's body and his hands upon it.

Taking Rebecca with him, he moved closer to Abigail. Reached for the vial of thick oil beside her.

"Open your hands," he said to Abigail, then poured a few drops onto her palms. "Time does not wait."

Arla Dahl

She smoothed the oils over her hands, her fingers, slowly, languidly, coating them thoroughly. Her eyes grew dark, no longer unsure but steady and bold on his. And then she reached for the edge of her skirts, raising them, exposing the creamy length of her legs. The fabric, gathered and cascading at her waist, blocked his view of her sex, but not her touch as she wormed her hand beneath it. She questioned him with her eyes and he nodded, urging her to continue.

"Know your pleasure." He knew the moment her hand found her core for she gasped and swayed with a force so sudden he thought she might fall.

She reached back with her free hand and grasped the table, leaning her rump fully against it.

He slid his hand from Rebecca's thigh to her mons, settled his palm there above her nether lips, his fingertips resting lightly against them. If his cock lay there, he would grip it in his own fist, pump it tightly until his seed spilled from him. But it was not him, rather this tender one beneath his hand, her matted thatch moist with her juices. He pressed his palm more firmly to her mons, drew his fingers slowly up along her swollen lips then down again, pleased to note the tremors rippling through her as her body responded to this intimate touch. He pressed harder, held her tightly as she shivered and sighed.

"Touch her, Abigail," he said, "Touch her as you touch yourself."

Abigail reached out tentatively, the oil upon her hand glistening much like Rebecca's juices upon his fingers.

He grasped Abigail's small wrist and pressed her hand to Rebecca's mound. A shiver engulfed both women at the moment of joining. And then he covered Abigail's hand with his , guiding it, pulsing her fingers against Rebecca the same as if he guided Abigail's hand to pulse and pull and press against him.

He took in the movement of her skirts as her hand worked against her own heat in the same rhythm. Abigail's passion creased her brow, made her eyes glisten. The lips of her mouth swelled and he knew her nether lips swelled the same, dripped, ached for more than her hand to satisfy the need there, much as he ached for more to satisfy his.

And Rebecca sighed, her breaths heaving from her own swollen lips, the wet passion of her core clinging to his hand and Abigail's.

With a firm yet gentle touch, he smoothed his dampened hand up along Rebecca's body, let it flow into the curve of her waist, then flare out along her rib, her breast. He cupped her breasts then and caressed them. Seeing and feeling no mark on her pale slim body. Noting no hint of betrayal from her lips. Her sighs as true as Abigail's. Her trembling from need, not mischief.

He reached for Rebecca's nipples, spoke softly into Rebecca's ear, "Describe that which you feel," he said and gently tugged the small nubs. She leaned more fully against him, the heat of her body seeping through to his.

"I cannot." Her words came out on a breath so harsh, he feared she might find release from these first touches alone.

"You must for I will know if 'tis truth or lies for only the witch cannot feel."

"I...cannot take air," she said, "yet I do not feel faint..."

"What do you feel?" His eyes were on Abigail. His words were for Rebecca.

"I feel shamed…"

"There is no shame in pleasure, Rebecca," he said in a low murmur. "If it is pleasure you feel, I will hear of it."

"I…know not whether I chill or burn…" She shuddered and tensed, and Abigail did the same, her hands moving against the girl and herself in a frenetic way.

"Slow, Abigail," he said, skimming his hand lower to grasp Abigail's wrist and tame her ministering, not wishing either to find release at this moment, not yet while Rebecca still had much to prove.

Abigail stilled, her chest heaving, her eyes heavy.

Rebecca breathed hard, shifted against him, her rump grinding into his cock, making it convulse in pulses of excruciating bliss. Closing his eyes, he hissed a breath and held her tight, ceasing her movements against him so he might halt the flood of his own release.

He thought of the others, pictured them outside, bare, cold, waiting. Each needing to be examined, each afraid for their lives. He was their examiner. His vow was to prove their innocence or their guilt. Not to seek pleasure for himself. Yet Abigail taunted him with her sighs and shivers, and Rebecca, pressed so well against him, created need he could not easily ignore. But ignore he must. They awaited his word. It would free them. Or hang them.

Easing his hold on Rebecca, he reached for the pool of oil on the table. As he scooped more of it onto his fingers, Abigail's ministering started anew with a slow gentle dance against herself and Rebecca.

He smoothed his hand along Rebecca's hip, feeling only warm, damp flesh. Smooth, unmarked, alive. And then he slid his oiled fingers over the tense mounds of her rump and the space between them, waited not a moment and pressed against the tightness there, holding her more firmly against him with his other hand, breathing with her as her breaths grew sharp and quick.

"Feel what we do, Rebecca," he said.

Abigail continued her soft touches and he eased his finger past the tight ring that sought to block him. He held his finger there, a mere knuckle within Rebecca's anus, heard her whimper, welcomed all signs of her tormented pleasure, satisfied she felt this intimate intrusion.

He pushed on, eased his finger deeper inside of her, pleased by her sighs, her spasms. Her clenching need. He slid his free hand higher, over her waist, her breasts, to her neck, grasping her by the chin, tipping her head back to his shoulder. Not reprimanding her for her closed eyes or harsh wordless breaths. And then he pushed further into her, sliding his finger deeper, not stopping until he was to the web of his fingers, pressed firmly and fully within. He twisted his wrist, circling his finger inside of her, feeling her body tense further. Gripping him, not permitting him to withdraw, her body trembling against him as though her release teetered just beyond her reach.

"Abigail cease," he said and when she did, he eased his finger from Rebecca's tight heat, so gently, so slowly, her body tensed around him, claiming his finger for itself until he slid it free.

Rebecca cried out, a pitiful sound of want and need.

Abigail stood back. Her breath racing past her lips. Her hand slowly falling to her side. Her release clearly as close as Rebecca's. Her need as great as his.

He set a hand low on Rebecca's back, urged her forward toward he table, pushing until her chest pressed the wood. He could not permit her release. Could not grant her pleasure until he was certain all of her lay unmarked.

"Widen your stance," he said, and pushed her feet apart with his. "Further," he said with more force, hoping to distract her from the pleasure her body still felt, watching her as she moved, assuring himself that nothing, not the table's edge nor her own sweet dripping lips would caress her or satisfy her need. "Clasp your hands low at your back and remain there."

She did as she was told and he settled his gaze on Abigail, her distress as evident as Rebecca's. Her body trembling, her breaths unsteady. Her hands shifting, first clasped together then free at her sides.

"You will find leather straps there," he said and pointed where they rested upon a shelf mounted on the wall above the table. "Secure one to each of the four irons."

Understanding flickered past Abigail's darkened eyes and he turned away, certain the memory of what would befall Rebecca next was clear in Abigail's mind. Though it would be different for Rebecca than it had been for Abigail. Rebecca's purity was clear, her need, her scent not as compelling.

He dared not glance back at Abigail for even fully clothed, her body called to him. It was not the time. He had tasted her – more than he should have, more than any before her. Yet he could do naught but think of having her again, of tasting her fully, of touching her. Taking her.

The sound of his own breaths, his own blood coursing painfully through him, was loud in his ears. Insistent. Steady as his step as he went to the hearth to wash all traces of the oil and Rebecca from his fingers.

Hastily he dried his hands on a cloth by the hearth, then grasped his erection through his breeches. He squeezed himself painfully, forcing the ache, the need, to pass unfulfilled, for this was not how it was meant to be. Not with thoughts of Abigail, but rather with thought of the others' arousal. It was that which he sought. Their awareness, their responses. Not his own pleasure. Not his own release.

Able to breathe fully once again, he eased his hand from his cock. Then he smoothed his breeches flat so the women might not know of his weakness. With barely a glance their way, he went to the chest and retrieved cloths and a sharpened blade.

Back at the table, he tested the restraints Abigail had tied there, noted how she watched his every move. Even as he set the blade onto the shelf, she watched, her breath quick, her eyes unsure. The want she displayed just moments prior, shrouded by the same doubt and discomfort he had noticed from her earlier.

He lifted the blade, rolled the handle between his fingers it until the metal glinted in the candlelight.

She blinked as though awakened, cut her gaze from the blade to him.

"Take up the vials," he said. "Bring them and Rebecca to me."

She turned away quickly, as if seeking reason to move about, and he understood where her thoughts had gone. She, like he, recalled when she lay spread and bound to the table, the restraints keeping her in place. She would recall, too, the feel from each stroke of the blade against her. Of his fingers, slick from the oils and her juices, as he shaved her mons and labia clean. As he tested them, as he slid his fingers along their swollen length, spread them... searched for the mark, hoping she would feel his every touch and respond as an innocent would.

The women stood before him, rousing him from his musings.

Abigail's face was flushed near the same as Rebecca's. He pressed a palm to Rebecca's cheek, felt the heat there. Smoothed his thumb along it to her jaw. Noting the desire, the fear in her eyes, and wanting to reassure her. To reassure Abigail.

"You are meant to feel as you do now," he said to Rebecca.

"I know of these sensations..." Her voice was soft but steady, showing restrained, not sinful, pride. "But never have I felt them... and should not feel them now." Though her body trembled, her gaze remained on his.

"Unless you are marked, you will feel more," he said, noting how her eyes widened, her breath hitched. "But I assure you," he continued with a slight conceding tip of his head, "should I find you unmarked, you will find release." He slid his gaze to Abigail as she lifted a hand to her throat and closed her eyes.

"Set the vials here, Abigail," he said, and pointed to a spot at the narrow edge of the table. She did as told and he extended his hand to Rebecca. "You are near through," he said, then used his foot to ease a small stool out from beneath the table.

The girl hesitated only a moment then placed her cold hand in his and stepped onto the stool.

"Sit at the table's edge," he said and held her hand until she did so. "You will lie back." He waited for her to do as he bid then bent to remove her slippers. "I will position you," he said, "and you will not resist." He grasped her ankles. "Do you understand?"

"Good Sir."

It was not time for Abigail to intrude. It was time for Rebecca to hear only his voice. To feel only his touch. She would know of nothing but her own nakedness. Would be aware only of her body, of how it felt and how it appeared to his eyes.

Abigail would recall this moment, would recall the cravings created by it. He recalled as well and had fought against them himself with each of the accused who lay bare and spread before him.

Each except Abigail.

He raised Rebecca's legs, allowing the natural bend at her knees as he set her heels upon the table. "You have merely been touched here this night," he said, then smoothed his palms along the inside of her thighs, urging them apart. "You will now be seen."

Chapter Four

Jameson took the smaller of the two vials Abigail had set on the table and poured a few drops of its fragrant oil into his hand. He warmed it between his palms, then spread it, hand over hand, along the silken flesh of Rebecca's inner thigh, gently easing her leg further to the side with each caress, moving it closer to the corner where he secured her ankle with the leather strap. With only a brief glance at Abigail to see she still watched, he repeated the same on the other side, spreading Rebecca and securing her until her swollen and weeping nether lips were fully exposed to his view.

"Good Sir?"

"Secure her wrists," he said, purposely interrupting Abigail so she might not distract Rebecca with chatter.

Abigail moved slowly, almost cautiously, and he spared her a quick glance, curious for her thoughts, though he would not inquire, for this time was for Rebecca alone.

The girl whimpered but did not struggle as Abigail lifted her arm above her head to secure it to the restraint at the far corner.

He went to Rebecca's side, saw fear in her eyes as she looked up at him, though if he had doubt of her terror, the mottled flush on her face and her chest proved his assessment true. He cupped a hand to her forehead, smoothed it over her hair.

"The restraints are not to frighten you," he said as Abigail secured her other wrist. "They are to keep you from moving so no blood is drawn."

Tears rushed to fill her eyes and a rippling breath lifted her chest.

He shook his head slowly and offered her a small smile, not wishing for her to suffer undo worry. "Have you been harmed here this night?" he asked softly.

She opened her mouth as if to speak, but no words came from her. Slowly she rocked her head side to side.

"You chose this fate to prove innocence," he said, "did you not?"

She nodded, her gaze unwavering.

He cupped his other hand gently to her throat, skimmed it down to her chest, felt the rapid flutter of her heart as it pounded beneath his palm. And then he cupped her breast, gently caressed it, lightly squeeze it, never shifting his gaze from hers. Watching closely, noting the flare of her nostrils and slight crease of her brows.

He grasped her nipple lightly. Held it. Tugged. Kept his smile of satisfaction from forming when she whimpered, for it was his hope to coax her desire once more.

"I would know if you are marked," he said, giving her this opportunity to confess if it be so.

She did not speak, merely shook her head.

He gave one more small tug on her nipple, then released it and eased his hand lower, skimmed it over her belly, her mons, and let his fingers slide gently between her labia until he felt the moisture that still lingered there.

A tremor rippled through her and her eyes widened as if in shock, fear, and pleasure. An innocent's response to such a touch.

"I...am not marked," she said in a pained and ragged whisper. "But I know not how to prove my innocence."

"I will see you," he said, ignoring the tears and pleading in her eyes. This moment above all could reveal the truth, and he could not distract her, nor offer her comfort. "I will know of your secrets."

With the slightest shift, the lightest touch, he slid his hand upward, brushing his fingers through her slit until just the very tips of them wisped over her tiny hidden nub.

She cried out and joggled herself as much as the restraints would allow. He pulled his hand away, satisfied by her responses. Then he left her there, spread and bound, and went to the hearth to retrieve the kettle.

"Good Sir..." Abigail followed, stood beside him, her voice softer this time. "The women...outside..."

He brushed past her, settled the kettle on the table beside Rebecca, and carefully tucked a thick cloth between it and her flesh so she would not feel the heat overmuch.

"Surely they shiver," Abigail said as he adjusted the stool so it rested before Rebecca's spread legs. "Must they continue to suffer the cold and the crowd's scrutiny?"

He plunged several torn strips of cloth into the heated water, squeezed the excess from one. "What would you have me do?" he asked, keenly aware of the rising pitch of Abigail's voice.

"Allow them into the manor."

Rebecca's legs were splayed out before him, her mound awaiting his ministerings. With a shake of his head, he pressed the warm cloth flat to it. She jolted as though scalded, though he knew it was not so hot. "You must lie still," he said, and pressed another cloth there as well, softening the thatch of hair that covered her. He cupped his hand to it, containing its moist heat.

"Good Sir...if I may..."

He took the blade from the shelf then sat upon the stool before Rebecca legs and leaned in.

"Please... I...cannot..."

Abigail's chatter was a dangerous thing while he held a blade so sharp. He set it down and looked at her, wondered over the worry in her eyes. And then they shifted, seemed to brush over the girl's prone body, her legs, his hand resting on her mound, and he could not tell whether Abigail's discomfort came from her concern for the women outside or for the attention he would now pay Rebecca. "You cannot what, Abigail?"

"What you do here... now..." Her hand went to her throat and her chest heaved but it was not from arousal, rather, he thought, she might faint. "I cannot be of help," she said, "is that not true?"

He turned back to Rebecca, took the cloths from her mons and inhaled slowly, deeply, as Abigail had earlier when she indicated Rebecca's scent.

"You have done well with her this hour," he said still smelling a tinge of the girl's light scent in the air. He gave Abigail a small smile but she did not return it. "But, nay," he said, "this only I may do."

He turned back to the girl. Pinched one plush lip between his fingers, listened for her soft whimper, then slid his fingers down its length, permitting the slight shift of the girl's legs and hips as the touch stirred her. He pulled on that sweet lip, stretched it out and to the side, noted how her juices dripped from her and how that small pink, protruding nub begged for his attention.

"You may go, Abigail," he said without turning her way. "Have the watchman bring the others secured. I will see to Rebecca."

Abigail hurried from the room, the chamber door slowly creaking closed once she was through, then slamming as she opened the doors to the outside. He waited for the familiar clunk of the manor doors closing then lifted the blade.

"You must not move," he said, then gently, carefully, scraped the edge of the blade against Rebecca's mons, whisking away the coarse hairs that blocked a clear view of her flesh.

The slight rasp of the blade merged with the crackle of flames in the hearth, the sounds made less harsh by the gentle rhythm of their breaths. His, deep and steady so his hand would not jostle. Hers quivering with each minor adjustment he made, tugging her flesh taught to get every hair in one pass. Flattening her labia, pressing and stretching it firmly with his fingers so as not to catch the delicate skin with the sharpened edge.

His every touch was sure. Thorough. Aware. His senses alert to her responses, for each time he drew near her pinkened nub, she trembled, her need seeming to guide her more than her fear. Careful not to touch her overmuch, he spread her, looked closely at the glistening flesh of her thinner lips within, rippled and protecting her core. He moved the blade from her and used the pads of his thumbs to spread those tiny lips apart, allowing for the sudden jerk of her body.

"You are most responsive, Rebecca," he said when she whimpered. "This part of you, so tender and pink, swells and glistens even as I look upon of it." He spread her further, stretching her wide and felt his own body respond as her nub peeked further from beneath its shield, eager to be touched and soothed. A soothing he would not grant until certain of her purity.

Gently, he dipped a finger into her juices, more potent now as they freely wept from her. He brushed his finger against her opening, circling it, spreading her lips wider, stretching her maidenhead. And then he pressed his finger to it, testing it, feeling its slight flex, moist as it was from her arousal. Slowly, ever so carefully, he eased his smallest finger through the small natural tear there, just a touch, a breath at a time not wishing to cause her pain. She tensed, seem to have swallowed a cry as her thighs trembled and her belly quivered. He hesitated, gave her a moment to calm.

"Where I have looked, you have been unmarked..." He eased his finger in further, slowly, letting her body adjust to this small intrusion. Barely two knuckles within, he thought his finger too thick and feared her maidenhead might tear.

"Where I have felt..." He eased back just a bit, not wanting to spill her innocent blood. "...you have been untouched." To be sure he spoke the truth, he curled his finger, flexing and stretching it within her, feeling the smooth softness there. With each stroke of his finger, she writhed and whimpered and pulled at her restraints.

Needing no further proof that she was not marked there, her flesh not deadened, he eased his finger from her. Though a small sound came from her, like a squeal suddenly made silent, her maidenhead remained intact, and he knew then, without question, it had never been breached, neither by the beast nor gently so.

He slid his hand down toward her rump, then, and parted her buttocks so he might reach the feathery wisps at her tight and timid hole. He lifted the blade again and slowly drew it against her, making each movement there slight.

The flesh he exposed, dusky pink and puckered, was unmarked lest for one pin-tip of a blemish. He scraped it lightly with the blade and she quivered, responding as he would hope, proving the spot, too, was not dead.

He wiped her clean with a cloth, then sat back and looked at the bare flesh before him. Beautiful in its nakedness, with no teat nor devil's mark to mar it. He rinsed the blade in the kettle then set it safely upon the shelf. Hoping the rest of the examinations would lead to the same end.

"You have done well, Rebecca." He went to her side, smiled into her worried eyes. "You are unmarked."

She cried without tears, laughing softly as in relief, yet her body remained tense, and he understood.

He soothed her with a palm to her forehead, lightly stroked her. "Your body is warm, with a flush upon your breasts. Do you feel it?" He cupped her breast, gently probed it with his fingertips, pressing his thumb firmly to her nipple, rubbing it until her body shifted with want. She looked up at him, seeming unsure how to respond. "What is it you seek?" he asked, though he knew well the answer.

No words, only a soft sound, from high in her throat answered him. A sound of innocent yearning. He flattened his palm to her breast, smoothed it down to her belly and drew firm circles over her, slowly easing those circles lower. "You have suffered greatly this hour. The sensations you felt still heat you."

She whimpered but did not speak.

"I would ease this tension you feel," he said. "You have only to speak the words."

"I know not the words you seek."

He circled lower, rested the heel of his hand against her mons, let his fingers rest against her nub and lips, and made the circles smaller, slower. Feeling her flesh move beneath his hand, letting his fingers fall more solidly against her. "You need tell me to cease or keep on."

Her hips lifted to his hand, and though need etched deeply between her brows, she still did not speak the words.

He moved his hand lower, burying his fingers deeply between her outer lips, stroking those more sensitive hidden beneath, knowing what she wanted, what she needed and deserved, though unwilling to draw it from her without her plea or permission.

"You must have me stop, if that is your wish," he said, seeing how need seemed to cause her pain. "These next moments are for you alone." He spoke softly, slowly, wanting her to feel, to accept this time for herself. "They are for your choices and desires." He stilled his hand, pressed his fingers more firmly to her, felt her lips soak them, swallow them, and he knew he had only to brush his thumb to her nub and she would feel the release she did not yet know she craved.

"Do not stop," she said, her back bowing, her eyes closing. "Please... I know not the words..."

"You are free, Rebecca," he said, then slid his wet fingers up to her nub, three of them, and pressed them against her, drawing those circles slowly in one direction, feeling her tense, seeing her belly tighten. And then stopping just a moment for her to breathe, and circling them again the opposite way. Her breath swelled her chest as her body bowed further. And he resisted the urge to grasp himself with his free hand, stroke himself, hard and fast, to satisfy his own need. He eased his pressure, circled her slowly in both directions, unsteady with his strokes so each would feel new.

With a gasp, she opened her eyes, wide and pleading, as her hips rose to meet his hand more firmly. He obliged, giving her the pressured touch she sought, still circling her nub. And then he tapped his fingertips to it, once, twice, four times, six, ten... continuing as she cooed a long low sigh, her body writing as far as the restraints allowed. He held his fingers against her, rubbed her gently, taking all she had to give, not stopping only slowing, aware how even a tender touch could become too much when just a moment prior it had been not near enough.

She calmed, though breaths still shuddered from her.

He smiled down at her, smoothed his free hand over her head. Met her gaze when she opened her eyes. "You have earned this reward," he said. "And though you have felt this pleasure, there was no breach, you are still most pure."

Her deep breaths answered him. The flush that had covered her face and breasts faded. And he reached for the restraints at her wrists, released them one at a time, smoothing his hand over her arms, her shoulders, easing the ache she would feel there.

"Are you well?" he asked as he freed her ankles and soothed the stiffness from her legs.

She took his offered hand and sat up. "Aye," she said. "I... am free." Her small smile drew his.

"You are." He heard the doors to the manor open. "The others come," he said, then took her slippers from the floor and put them on her small cold feet.

Her eyes showed panic and she lifted her arms to cover her breasts. He took her hands in his as the door to the chamber opened, the calm fire-lighted air in the room suddenly chilled and busy with the shuffling of slippers and jangling of chains.

"You cannot hide now," he said to her, "but you will soon be clothed." He helped her to her feet, the move eliciting a collective gasp from the bound women now a mere yard within the room.

He looked at each of them. Their faces were flushed from the cold, their eyes wide and pitying as they looked at Rebecca, themselves nearly bare, though not yet shaved clean. Only the matron closed her eyes, herself seeming to pray. He looked to the watchman as he tethered one end of the irons to a shacklebolt on the wall.

"Giles."

The watchman turned and his gaze fell upon Rebecca, sliding head to slippers. And then he looked away, seemed unsure where to settle his eyes.

Jameson knew of no one else beyond himself and Giles to care for the women rather than see only guilt. They would be safe in his care. "They are to remain apart," he said to Giles. "Each bound alone." He looked at Abigail and saw a slight tearful smile upon her face. He nodded, assuring her that he had found Rebecca unmarked. "You will assist as he requests," he said to her, then led Rebecca past the women and into the hall.

"They will all see you now," he told Rebecca as they reached the doors to the yard. "But you have naught to hide for you are unmarked."

"I wish to be clothed," she said, her hands lifting to cover herself once more.

For these few private moments alone, he permitted her that modesty. Giving her a moment more to accept how bare she was as her hand fell to her mons. She knew now of the pleasures another's touch would bring. Soon she would know her own touch could bring the same. It showed in her languid eyes, eyes that no longer avoided his.

"We must go," he said, then opened the doors and offered his arm for her to hold.

They stepped outside together, her hand clutching him for the first few seconds. And then the crowd quieted, turned to face them, and she dropped her hand to her side, standing alone, proud. Seeming comfortable before all in only her slippers.

With his fingertips at her back, he led her down the stairs. "Who will clothe this innocent woman?"

A deafening cheer came from the crowd and then three women rushed forward with skirts and stays, and began to dress her.

He gave her a small bow as the women pulled her this way and that, covering her naked body with layers of white cotton. She smiled at him, a lovely smile, the first true happiness he witnessed from her this night.

Satisfied she was well cared for, he returned to the manor to find Giles in the hall, his black hood off his head, his hand scuffing his flattened hair.

"Will you be needing me further?" he asked as Jameson went to him.

"Not for some time," Jameson said pointing to the stairs leading up. "Should you seek slumber you may use—"

"Slumber will not come," Giles said in a tone that quivered to well mock those of the crowd, "when there be witches among us." He opened his eyes wide like those with the most terror, then closed them and donned his black hood once more.

Though he mocked, he did not smile and Jameson felt no humor either. The examinations were not new, the accusations too familiar, yet it seemed no one but for the accused, Jameson, and his knowing friend saw the madness of such happenings. Neighbor turning on neighbor. Father turning on mother.

Jameson pressed a hand to Giles' shoulder. "With mercy there will be no witches here this night."

"With your mercy..." Giles made for the doors, turning back when he opened them, "dawn will bring light..." he said and stepped outside, "for all those in your care." He gave a slight tip of his head and closed the doors between them.

Jameson went into his chamber, satisfied to see the women bound by one limb, not spread, not bared, their torn shifts modestly covering much of their charms. Abigail stood by the hearth, placing a new candle within a stick there.

A woman with warm reddish hair stood nearest to him. Elizabeth Hobbs. Her eyes had challenged him earlier, showing pride bold and strong. He would examine her first, then send her from these rooms before such behavior, should it appear again, afflicted the others.

He went to the table and lifted the kettle. "Abigail, you may release Elizabeth," he said, "And bring her here." He brought the kettle to the hearth, set it to heat and turned in time to see Elizabeth's eyes lift to his, steady. Brazen.

"Why are you here, Elizabeth?" he asked as Abigail set the restraints on the floor.

Elizabeth rubbed her wrists and slowly lifted her chin, never turning her gaze from his. "I have been unjustly accused of a crime I had never thought to commit."

"And you wish to prove your innocence..." They were the words he needed to hear. The words that permitted him to examine her, words that could free her, permit her to bare herself without shame and be touched. Seen. Proven unmarked. "...by submitting to me this hour."

"Nay," she said her chin still high. "That is not my wish."

The Accused

Chapter Five

As Jameson feared, defiance still danced within Elizabeth's eyes. He glanced at Abigail. Perhaps he had been unwise to permit her presence during these examinations. Certainly, he had been wrong to honor her request for the others to enter his chambers together.

He looked at them, their eyes expectant, unsure. He could not permit such disruption from Elizabeth or it would spread to all. He met Elizabeth's bold defiant gaze once more.

"If you do not wish to prove innocence," he said, "then you admit guilt."

"I am innocent." She waved a hand toward the others. "We are all innocent. It is madness and greed and vengeance which condemns us to these shameful trials and I am loathe to succumb to them. Nay. I will not submit."

Abigail went to Elizabeth, her hands clasped as if in prayer. "Elizabeth…you must… The governor will do all to prove to all that you are innocent…that you are all innocent… He will…"

The Accused

Jameson glanced back toward the door to the other chamber where those found marked would be further tested. He thought to bring Elizabeth there, to take her from this space. For peace. She would be bound and left alone, in that silent and darkened room. She would have time to think, to calm and not worry the others.

"He would treat me as a whore for his own pleasure," she said to Abigail. "Do you not see that?"

Others before her had resisted. Most he calmed and convinced, but it was through patience, not force. At this hour, with so many still to be examined, he had but little patience left.

"It is not true, Elizabeth." Abigail's patience was clear in her light tone and sensible words. She placed her hand on Elizabeth's arm, looked only at her. "What he does is for us, not himself."

"Did you not see Rebecca?" Elizabeth withdrew from Abigail's touch, her voice rising. She pulled her torn shift closer to her flesh, but the fabric, beyond repair, left the full swell at the side of her breast bare. Still she held it, her arm covering more of her than her shift.

She took a step toward the other women. "Did you all not see her?" She looked at them as though she had not a shred of sense, not an idea how eager they were to prove their innocence. They looked at her with more pity than understanding in their eyes.

"How do you yield to this man?" she said. "Bare yourselves to him and allow him to violate your bodies? Can you not see why he does this?"

Her breasts swayed as she moved. Her nipples hardened, poked at the thin fabric with every passionate phrase she uttered.

It took all of his control to keep from thrashing her, securing her body and mouth so she could not speak further nor cause the others to fret more. Once she relented, he would do all to prove her innocence…though her pride, her bold words and actions made him fear her innocence might not be proven.

She turned to him, her shift gaping at the breast though she still held it closed at the throat. Her passion and fire, her anger and pride were bold and sinful. He knew this yet his body betrayed his mind for, though he wished to deny it, she stirred him. Her full breasts and small waist called to all that was male within him. Not governor, not examiner. It was immoral. Lustful. Yet he was forced to stare, to watch her every move.

Her petticoats, damp from the cold outside air, clung to her hips and her full mound, the richness of her reddish hair darkening the thin fabric that barely covered her there. That fabric tapered down the length of her legs, long and lean they were, and he thought of them spread, bound upon the table. He would take care with her as with the others, though even if she were to submit, she would fight, she would challenge him, making restraint – of her and of himself – yet more difficult.

Would she find release at his hands? Would she allow herself that pleasure? Or would she resist that too, feign indifference to his touches no matter how drenched she became in her own juices….

"Look!" She pointed to his breeches, her eyes wide. "See how this arouses him!"

He could grip himself and squeeze all pleasure from him. Instead, dipped his head in a small bow, conceding her point.

"I am a man oftimes betrayed by my own body," he said. "But as your governor, your examiner, I will not be betrayed by my mind." He turned to the others, made the vow as much for them as for himself. "Nor any of you."

He walked slowly past each of them, looking not at their bodies but into their eyes, hoping they would accept the truth and promise of his words. "It is not your honor I wish to prove, it is your purity. It is not your virtue I wish to save. It is your lives. I would not offer my service if it were otherwise."

"What?" Elizabeth laughed. A sound almost like that of madness. "Would you have us believe that? Do you believe our gender renders us dense? Do you, Abigail?"

"Elizabeth, please..."

"Do you not see what he does here?"

"...there are but few hours..."

"Or are you blind? So enamored by his charm, so weakened by his touch that you would yield even your thoughts?"

He could stop all of this in an instant, but to what end? He had permitted her to go on too long and she had now frightened the others. And not only fear worried their eyes but doubt, for she had given them cause to question his abilities and his intent.

If he could force her from these rooms, he would. But to do so would rouse rebellion in the others, and they would follow.

That, he would not allow. It would be his failing. It could be their end.

Abigail approached Elizabeth slowly, as if she, too, struggled to remain calm.

"I posses my own thoughts," she said, answering Elizabeth's challenge. "They are the property of no one. My body is my own as well but it would not have been had I not yielded, for I would have been at the mercy of the crowd. Did you not see them? Did you not hear them? Were you not stripped to the waist and paraded before them?" She turned to the other women. "Were all of you not examined by them, shamed and sickened by their touch?"

The others agreed. Martha closed her eyes and seemed to pray. Hannah's eyes brimmed with unshed tears. Only Mercy remained as stone. Observing while giving no sign of her thoughts.

"They are greedy and filthy," Abigail said. "They would touch you for their pleasure. They would mock you and seek to prove you marked by the beast." She turned back to Elizabeth. "But our governor… he seeks to prove our innocence." She silenced Elizabeth with a raised hand. "'Tis not fair," she said softly. "But, 'tis my promise to you that he is kind and merciful."

"Kind and merciful?" Elizabeth's voice rose yet higher in pitch. "Ha! Look at dear Hannah! She trembles in fear and shame. Yet he will violate her body and you declare that kind and merciful? Come!" She urged Hannah to her, her hand outstretched in offering. Hannah had but to reach for it with her unbound hand. "Come Hannah, you need not betray your honor to have your innocence proven. They will see you are unmarked."

Hannah's eager eyes betrayed her thoughts, and Jameson went to her, blocking her view of Elizabeth.

He bowed his head slightly, lowering his voice to a most gentle tone. "It is your choice, Hannah. It has been from the start." Pleased his words came without anger, he went on. "You may submit to me, here within these walls, where I will do all in my power to prove your innocence. Or you may leave. Stand naked before that crowd..." Her eyes grew frightened and he forged ahead caring not that she cried. "...and have each of them – all of them – touch you. Examine you."

He glanced at the others. "I have seen what they can do," he said, then turned back to Hannah, capturing her gaze once more. "They will search you everywhere, every crevasse, every secret spot, and if they cannot find what they seek, they will hold you down and spread you wide to search your naked body further. Why do you weep, Hannah? Is that not the choice you would make?"

Hannah trembled before him, her tears falling unchecked. "It is no choice... I am afraid..."

"See what you do to her?" Elizabeth's sharp tone fell to a vehement hum. "You are an animal, yet you treat her as one, so eager are you for her to lay at your feet, with no regard for her needs, her fears. You want only pleasure for yourself."

He moved not, still blocking so Elizabeth might not be seen. "Is that what you believe, Hannah?"

Hannah studied him, and he permitted it, despite the passing time.

"I am innocent," she said.

"How shall it be proven?" he asked, stepping aside so he no longer blocked her view, for the choice was hers to make. "Will you go with Elizabeth or will you stand here, with the others?"

She set her tear-filled eyes on Elizabeth, trembling, pleading. And then she closed her eyes, pressed the tears from them, and took a slow step backward, her shackles clanking as she moved. Abigail went to her, circled the woman's shoulders with an arm, soothing her.

Jameson turned away, unsure how Elizabeth might see the wisdom of Hannah's choice. He knew only how difficult this was for the accused, and that Elizabeth had made it yet more so, her misplaced pride most harmful to them and to herself.

"Morning does not wait, Elizabeth." He went to the table, faced her as he sat back against the edge, lifting a foot to rest it upon the stool and clasping his hands loosely atop his lap. "You must choose quickly," he said. "And wisely."

"I will never submit."

He could permit no further disruption. "We have not the time." He looked at Abigail, did all to conceal his distress from her and the others. "Fetch the watchman." The coarseness of his voice betrayed him. "Have him bring the irons."

With a gasp, Abigail rushed toward him. "No, Good Sir... please..."

He pushed to his feet. Stared down at her. "You will fetch him," he said, his jaw clenched to keep himself from shouting at her. "Now."

She hurried to the door, turned back with a pained and pleading expression. He did not blink nor look away until she rushed outside. He went to Elizabeth then, not stopping even as she stood back from him. She tugged the torn bits of her shift closer to her breasts. He did not stop her. These would be her last moments of modesty. Brief though they would be should she continue down this prideful and stubborn path.

"Think long, Elizabeth," he said. "No harm will come to you within this room."

Tears surfaced in her eyes. Whether caused by fear or by anger, he did not know.

"I would defend my life today," she said, "and my honor tomorrow? How, if my honor be questioned for yielding to you now? Nay. I will never submit."

A great clatter came from the hall. The manor doors had opened. Heavy boot steps, steady and unhurried, came in with a rush of cold air and garbled sounds, both of Abigail's worried murmur and the harsh grumblings of the crowd.

Abigail rushed in, stopped beside Elizabeth. The watchman remained at the doorway."

"Take her," Jameson said.

"Good Sir... please..."

The urgency of Abigail's voice touched deep in his heart. But he could do naught. He did not look at her. Did not remove his gaze from Elizabeth's.

Abigail turned to her. "Do not do this, Elizabeth."

Jameson motioned for the watchman. "Giles. Now."

The irons clanged angrily as Giles shackled Elizabeth's hands behind her. She did not resist or cry out, though the other women whimpered. Even when Giles' hand closed over her arm and turned her toward the door, she did not relent.

Jameson took a step toward them. "Wait there," he said, then turned to Abigail. "Fetch the heavy tow-cloth pouch from within the chest, and give it to him." Abigail was slow to move until he spun on her, silent but firm in his command.

Giles stood with Elizabeth at the door. Jameson went to them, stopping only when his chest touched Elizabeth's rigid back. And then he leaned into her softness, spoke quietly so only she might hear. "Will you not reconsider?"

"I will not."

He hesitated, wishing the words to end this madness would come to him.

He eased back from her, then pulled her torn shift back down to her elbows, baring her breasts once again. She gasped but did not speak, and he turned her to face him. Purposely lowered his gaze to her plush naked beauty, forcing appreciation from his expression, leering at her as the crowd would do, giving her a sense of what was to come. And then he reached behind her, bringing his doublet in contact with her stiff little nipples as he tugged the shift further down, forcing it to the shackles at her wrists.

"By refusing to submit to me," he said, then turned her toward the hall again, "you knowingly and freely submit yourself to the crowd."

She made a sound but not a word.

He waved a hand at the watchman. "Take her away."

He locked his gaze on the empty doorway well after she was led through. Slowly, as though drawn, he went to it, bowing his head, wishing for the words to change her mind as the watchman took her outside. The rumbling chatter of the crowd slowly fell to a low hum then grew silent. And then Giles' voice rang out, clear and strong.

"Who will examine this woman?"

The sudden roar was deafening, maddening. The crowd too eager to oblige.

Jameson stepped back into the room and closed his chamber door, turning to face the others. Their frightened eyes lowered as he dared them to speak. "If such nonsense still exists within these walls," he said, "I will hear it now."

Silence answered him and he stormed over to them, doing all to ignore the rumble resounding still from the yard. He reached for Hannah and she withdrew. He would have no more of this. He snatched her arm, ignored her struggles as he removed her restraints and dragged her to the table.

"Good Sir!"

Abigail would free them all without testing. "Please..." She kept pace with him, her words spilling from her. "I, too, fear for Elizabeth. Must I fear for the others as well?"

He spun on her as he had before, his grip still tight on Hannah's arm. He saw the concern and the fear in Abigail's eyes but would not be swayed. Could not. "Bring the vials."

She did not move.

"Time. Abigail."

"Good Sir..." She touched her hands to his arm. "Jameson..." Her small hands were cold. "You thought me marked," she said, "then proved me pure..."

"You forget your place, Abigail."

She loosened her grip but did not let go, her hands warming against him, heating him. "I remember my place quite well," she said softly, "for it was a mere hour past when I was naked and spread here before you. I feared for my soul. I knew not how you would test me to prove my innocence, and when you doubted my purity, I feared for my life."

He had thought her marked, himself bewitched...

"The others are as frightened as I had been," she said, her bold gaze unwavering. "More now as they worry for Elizabeth. I offered my help so you might complete your task before the reverend arrives at daybreak." As she spoke, she skimmed her hand down his arm. Her touch left a heated path in its wake. Her eyes, sincere and pleading, captivated him. Her hand covered his as he held Hannah. "If you frighten them needlessly, distract them with your anger, they will not respond as they should and you will doubt them. Then you will be forced to test them again. As you did me. But daylight will not wait."

Shouts and cheers came from outside, louder than before. The crowd's hunger as yet unsated. He feared for Elizabeth, hated that he had failed her. But pride such as hers was a wicked thing and the villagers... they would see it stripped from her as easily as they would strip her clothes and her honor...

He loosened his hold on Hannah. "Take her," he said to Abigail. "You will see that she disrobes."

The Accused

Chapter Six

From atop the manor stairs, Elizabeth saw the full size of the crowd. The fury in their faces. The fear. All were made more vicious by the swirling smoke and fiery glow of their torches.

She struggled to remain poised, as Abigail had been when the governor displayed her before all. But Abigail would be declared innocent. Here, now, the watchman would encourage the mob to strip her, examine her. Test her flesh for the mark.

"I will not submit," she said, shocked by the harsh choking sound of her own voice.

"Why did you refuse?" The watchman stood behind her, his hard hands tight on her naked upper arms. "He would have spared you this."

"To submit to him would be to shame myself."

"They will not mind your virtue. They will take it. Is that not shame?"

"Faceless hands cannot shame the same as his."

"That is a fool's logic, Elizabeth." He drew a long breath, then bellowed. "Who will examine this woman?"

There was no time to think, to react, to relent. He urged her forward, down the stairs, over the grass to the gate. Her feet seemed to glide over the ground as he moved her ahead of him.

She would not resist. She would prove her innocence. Their want was to take from her but they would not. She would give. To them, not to the governor, for what he demanded was her body, her mind. What she offered the crowd was mere proof of her innocence.

Three women rushed toward her. They talked at once. Tugged at different parts of her clothing. Courage failed her and she recoiled, shouted at them to unhand her, heard the watchman tell her to cease, that to resist would make it worse.

Her tattered shift was torn from her bound wrists and tossed aside. Her foot was lifted, first one then the other, and her slippers discarded. The grass was cold, slick and wet beneath her feet. Hands tugged at the drawstring of her petticoats then latched onto the band at her waist. She clenched her legs together, not letting the garment slip past her hips. Other hands pulled at it, tearing it from her body, and she could do naught to stop it. But to stop it, to stop them, would be to accept guilt, and that she would not do.

As madness spiraled around her, the watchman spoke calmly in her ear. "I will not let them harm you, Elizabeth, but I cannot stop them from seeing you or touching you or having you."

She meant to reply but only a whimper escaped her, and she dropped her head back to the solid heat of his shoulder.

"They will examine all of you," he said, "or they will declare you stained."

She heard the governor's words, then, clear as if he spoke them in her ear again at that moment.

"You knowingly and freely submit yourself to the crowd."

They would not take what she did not give. "I submit," she said forcing her breaths to slow. "I will let them see me." She looked up at the sky, thought of an hour when this would be done and by decree she would be deemed unmarked. "I will prove my innocence."

The hands were gone from her. Only icy damp air touched her as it washed over her now naked body.

She shivered. "I will prove my innocence."

The watchman urged her forward, whispering to her as they moved closer and closer to the mob. "You must not fight." He took her beyond the gates, past the crowd, to a platform topped by a beam with shackles hanging from it. "I must give you to them…"

"I will prove my innocence."

"…but I will not turn away. Elizabeth?"

She let him lift her arms and lock her wrists to the irons above her head. The crowd had turned; all stood before the platform, staring. The manor, with all its dark secrets, stood far ahead of her.

She had chosen poorly. But she had chosen. "They will not take what I do not give freely."

"Calm, Elizabeth. Turn your eyes to me."

She shifted her gaze to the watchman's. Had to blink several times to see him clearly.

"You will be safe, you will look at me." He did not turn away, and she felt drawn to his eyes, soothed by them.

She nodded. Accepting his comfort.

"A witch cannot feel. They will make certain you do." Before she could respond, he turned his back to her and faced the crowd. "We begin," he said to a clamor of approval. "Be this a witch?"

Men and women climbed onto the platform from all sides. She could not see around them.

"Her flesh must be pure to sight and touch."

She heard the watchman but could not see him as hands reached for her, touched her. Some caressed her raised arms, some cupped her breasts. Some tender, some cruel and cold. They smoothed over her bare rump, slapped it, pinched her thighs, pushed the hair from her face and touched her cheek, her jaw, her neck.

"I will prove my innocence," she said, over and over.

And then the watchman was there. Shoving people aside. Demanding order.

Standing beside her, he lifted her hair and invited them to look at her, touch her, seek the mark but not mark her themselves.

Faces blurred before her eyes, the hands of one seemed to come from another. Though she tried to remain silent, she heard her own whimper as her body was pushed and pulled and rocked. Only the irons kept her from swaying too far. Then fingertips brushed her side from waist to hip, the touch so gentle a tremor of dread coursed through her.

Hands gripped her legs then, and forced her stance wide. She trembled, closed her eyes.

"The mark may be hidden," someone said as fingernails scraped down her inner thigh.

"Look to me, Elizabeth."

The voice was hushed. Calm. She searched for its source.

More hands were on her legs, rough, demanding, skimming down to her feet, spreading her toes, kneading her thighs from hips to knees, and she was spread further, her arms straining as the irons held them firm. And then fingers gripped her nether lips, pinched them, peeled her wide, opened her to frigid air and lurid stares. Hot breath mingled with the night mist. Fingers plied her wider, squeezed her labia, stretched it.

She tried to pull away from the touch, but hands she could not see caught her from behind, kneaded her cold quivering rump, spread her cheeks wide until she felt split from rear to core.

No part of her lay hidden, untouched. Even the mist seemed to caress and probe her as her body grew weak and moist.

And then someone's cold fingers invaded her core, slowly at first, to a knuckle perhaps. Then deeper. She felt herself stretched and softened, as the fingers grew warm within her. They pulsed inside of her. Forced an immodest cry from deep in her throat. Her body clenched around them even as they pulled out.

She rolled her head side to side, wishing for pain, not these touches meant to arouse. To be so exposed, so forcefully awakened before all, was shame too great to bear. She closed her eyes. If a witch could not feel, they should know she was not one, for her body quivered with her every breath.

The fingers invaded her once more, more forcefully now, then withdrew and entered her again. And a warm slippery finger touched her from behind as well. It pressed firmly where it should not, and every muscle within her grew so taut she ached.

It was no use. The finger pushed on until it eased through the tightness there, showing no mercy.

Slowly stretching her. Heating her. Filling her. Deeply. She would not scream, would not sigh. Could not bear for the crowd to see their effect on her. Yet it was only by submitting that she would be freed.

"I will see your eyes, Elizabeth."

She struggled to open them, to look to the watchman but could not.

Every twitch of her hips, sent the fingers deeper. No matter which way she recoiled from one touch, the other probed further until she was impaled both front and back, held in place by these fingers, rocking within her, sliding in and out. Forcing her heated body to tense and pulse.

Need rose within her, shame burned her face. And then the fingers behind her pulled out with a sudden tug that left her body eagerly clutching at nothing. She gulped in air, let her head lag backward and then the fingers behind entered her again, slowly, steadily, and she heard her own cry, like a hungry cat mewling.

"Look to me."

The fingers left her and another hand caressed her breast, flicked her nipple. She mewed again, unable to keep silent. Unable to deny her body's response to this relentless and immoral pleasuring.

"Elizabeth. Look to me."

She forced her eyes open. Saw the watchman beside her, close, his gaze steady on hers, his hand gentle on her breast.

"You will clasp the chains," he said calmly. "Or you will be hurt."

The words did not sound clear. Nothing was clear but the hands on her, now cupping her rump, holding her. And then her legs were lifted and she felt she would fall as all her weight pulled at her shackled wrists.

The watchman's arm came around her, tight beneath her breasts, his chest against her side, and he, along with the hands below, lifted her, held her.

"Clasp the chains," he said and she fumbled to reach for them above the shackles. "Do not let go."

She held tight, and he released her. Her muscles shook, straining to hold her own weight as her legs were raised higher. Her feet were touched, her calves caressed and scratched.

Her legs were spread wider and though she feared intent, she did not resist, but kept her gaze on the watchman's. Blue like a summer sky. Blue like the jay. Blue...

Something cold and hard was pressed between her legs as it demanded entry. She looked down to see hands on her everywhere, and a solid stone phallus being pushed into her.

"Look here, Elizabeth. Look here."

She glanced up at him, then back to where oils were poured and spread between her legs. She loathed the touches and the eyes upon her, yet they made her crave, made need overpower and resistance fade.

His arm went around her again, at her back, holding her as her muscles gave way. His free hand returned to her breast, his fingers rough against her nipple. He pinched it, pulsed his fingers tightly to it, making it throb and grow.

The phallus slid deeper and she felt herself open to it, accept it, only to have it quickly withdrawn and plunged into her again. Her body clenched around it, warmed to it. Seemed to draw it deeper inside.

"Only the witch cannot feel." He released her nipple, gripped the other the same as the first.

She looked at him, did not close her eyes. Did not look at the others, at any of those around her, touching her, spreading her, forcing her to feel not just fear but a shameful hot aching desire.

The phallus was withdrawn again and her body throbbed and sought it.

"'Tis wrong," she said even as her body begged for more.

"'Tis wrong to hide what you feel. Show them, Elizabeth." He leaned closer to her, dipped his head, took her nipple into his mouth, the fabric of his hood, fluttering against her breast as he suckled, laved. The wet heat was a new sensation, one that tingled at the source, fluttered and spasmed down to where the phallus gained entry once more. He scraped his teeth against her nipple. Pulled away.

"Show them," he said then smoothed his hand down her belly, to her nether lips. Her body quivered as his fingers nestled between them, their roughness scraping against her in delicious and wicked ways. Lovers shared touches such as these in darkness. They exchanged private sighs and shivers. Here, before all, she sighed. Shivered. Craved the rolling boil of pleasure that hid beyond shame. Wished it away as it hovered and dared her to reach for it. Tormenting her with its guise of something good, something whole. Something right for her to accept.

He held her open and nodded to someone out of her view. Warm fingers pinched her sensitive nub and she screamed with the shock and pleasure of it.

"Good, Elizabeth." His voice sounded forced. Tight. As tight as her belly. And she felt the first ripple of abandon pulse within her.

His fingers spread her wider, and the pinch came again.

Her breath caught in her chest and she beseeched him with her eyes, unable to speak. To stop the pleasure from peaking.

He nodded, his gaze steady on hers. "Show them."

The phallus filled her once more and her entire body tensed for one agonizing moment of bliss as sinful lust tempted her with pleasures just beyond her reach. It quickened her heart and stalled her breath until she feared she might faint. And then release came and she shook with unimaginable force as wave after wave of tight burning pleasure coursed through her, drew the phallus in deeper, tugging its thick bulging tip up to her womb.

"There! It is the mark!"

The fingers were gone, the waves still pulsed, her empty body grasped, begged, for the phallus that was no longer there. She trembled, blind and breathless. Pleasure tormenting her as it lingered, craved one more touch.

Voices grew deafening; her legs were dropped, spread.

"She bears the mark!"

"It's Satan's stain!"

She breathed. Heard. Cleared her vision. "No." Weak and suddenly chilled again, she searched for the watchman as more people stormed the platform. She could not find him, could not see him. Saw only those who crowded her, grabbed at her and gaped at something on her inner thigh even as her body quaked and recovered.

"I felt it, I felt it all." Every touch of their cold clammy hands. Their probing. The oils. The maddening curls of lust deep inside of her. A witch could not feel. "I am unmarked."

"Cease!"

She breathed in relief as the crowd parted and the watchman stood before her.

"I am unmarked."

His gaze met hers only briefly before he knelt at her feet.

The crowd drew closer, circled him, stared unabashedly at her as he held her thigh in one hand and probed it with the other.

"Do you not see it?" There was panic in the voice.

"She has lain with the beast!" Panic and fury.

He released her slowly then stood but did not meet her gaze. "There lies a mark upon your flesh."

People shouted as they rushed hither and yon. "Fetch the governor!" Some raced back toward the gate, some on to the manor. "He must be told!"

Voices jumbled. Rose to a crescendo. Silenced her desperate pleas. And the watchman turned away.

Chapter Seven

Abigail turned Hannah's naked back toward the glow of candles on the wall. Gently, she combed her fingers through Hannah's lush flaxen hair, brushing it to the side until it rested it in front of her shoulder.

How this timid and frightened thing could be twin to the bold and shameless Mercy, now lying beneath Jameson's blade, Abigail did not know. Hannah had trembled, much as Abigail herself, when Jameson bade her disrobe and then lie upon the table. Yet Mercy bared herself to him with no aid and with scant hesitation.

He had not prepared the twins with slow touches or caresses. Had not aroused their senses with the oils or tender attentions. He wanted them bare. He wanted all of them bare.

And as Abigail had watched, worried for Hannah's safety as Jameson's anger for Elizabeth had still been high, the tension of his hand on the blade abated.

His ministering grew ever so gentle as he shaved the small hairs from Hannah's core.

It seemed he found calm from the act. As though the blade was a reminder of his solemn duty to all of the accused, not merely to one whose choice was poor.

And here Hannah stood. Cold, bare and shaved. Trembling still beneath Abigail's searching fingertips. While Mercy, spread wide, sighed and cooed as though heated by hearth and hand. Jameson's hand.

Every deliberate scrape of his blade against Mercy's flesh was a slice to Abigail's heart, though it should not be. Jameson did not belong to her. Not this night. Mayhap not ever. He was governor to all, and each of the accused sought his attention, lest they be thrown to the crowd same as Elizabeth.

Abigail blinked as tears misted her eyes. Her heart hurting for Elizabeth, her mind confused by the pain cutting through her as Jameson tended Mercy.

She focused on her task. Smoothed her fingertips lower on Hannah's back, a hair's width before the generous swell of Hannah's rump, noting no devil's mark anywhere. No deadened flesh. Only gentle responses to the slightest touch, and shivers to those more bold.

She skimmed one finger along the curve of Hannah's waist. The caress pebbled Hannah's flesh and made her tremble more. She should be nearer the hearth, for warmth and light, but Abigail could not bear to stand there, so close to Jameson, while he sat but a breath from Mercy's essence.

Mercy gasped in that instant. A harsh sound that ended on a moan. Abigail and the others gasped in response. Even Martha, still bound, clothed and with eyes lowered, looked up with concern.

"My regrets, Mercy." Jameson spoke quickly, moved quickly. "It is slight." He stood and pressed a damp cloth between Mercy's legs. "Are you well?" Specks of blood tinged the cloth when he pulled it away.

Mercy remained still, her eyes softly closed. "Aye," she said with more contentment than fear or pain. "I am well."

Jameson's gaze lingered on Mercy, her back arched, her breasts lifting with each slow deep breath she drew. And then he shifted his gaze to Abigail.

She did not look away, but met it fully. Her need for that small bit of attention was great, for he had not spared her the slightest glance or encouraging word since ordering her to help Hannah disrobe.

She had thought him too aware of Mercy. Of Mercy too settled there, seeming to crave yet more of his touches, not ache to hide or shield herself from his eyes. But the darkness she expected in his gaze, the arousal from Mercy's sighs and pliant body, did not show itself. Only an odd sadness lay in their dark depths.

Abigail wrapped her arms around Hannah, hoping to draw his attention to her hands as she skimmed them up to Hannah's breasts. Gently, she molded them with her palms, not worrying how they spilled over, just taking pleasure in the feel of her, seeking to give pleasure as well, so Jameson might feel relief from Hannah's responses. He did not look at Hannah's breasts, but at Abigail, and then he turned wearily back to Mercy.

He worried for Elizabeth. He worried for all of the accused. Concern was in his every breath. Abigail had naught to fear from Mercy.

Though Mercy, should she offer herself too well, might have much to fear, for an innocent woman, one not so tempted by the pleasures of the flesh as she, would not raise such doubt or concern. Abigail knew. Her own responses had enraged Jameson, making his examination of her yet more grueling.

With a shudder of both pleasure and shame, she turned her attention back to Hannah.

She rested her chin on Hannah's shoulder, greedily devoured Hannah's breasts with her hands. Much larger than Rebecca's, they rested heavily against Abigail's palms, overflowed. They were fuller, softer. So much more to touch, to examine. To pleasure. Hannah's nipples were dark pink, not pale, as if they had already been tested, teased and repeatedly struck by Jameson's crop.

Abigail pinched them tightly, waited for Hannah's moan. And when it came from deep in Hannah's throat, Abigail gently rolled them between her fingers. And then she pinched them again, alternating the touches. Finding herself writhing against Hannah as Hannah did against her. Abigail's own need persisted, despite her body being clothed, her own breasts untouched.

"It is good to feel, Hannah," she said, not releasing those firm and lovely nipples from her grasp. "I would hear more of your sighs."

She skimmed her hands lower, over Hannah's slight belly and on to her lush thighs. Stroking the flesh there with her fingertips, scratching at it ever so lightly with her nails. Welcoming Hannah's squirming. Eager for yet more.

She urged Hannah toward the table as Jameson released the restraints holding Mercy there. And as he replaced the slippers on Mercy's feet, Abigail reached for the vial of rosemary oil beside them.

She poured a few drops into her hands and the fragrance filled her with longing. With need. Her body still carried its scent, still tingled as though Jameson's strong gentle hands lingered upon her, spreading it over her breasts, her thighs…

She did the same now to Hannah, smoothing it over her flesh until it glistened, until every stroke against it, every caress, would be like a thousand hands on her everywhere at once. Hannah sighed much the same as Abigail had, and Abigail reached for Hannah's core, needing to know the truth of Hannah's responses.

As she dipped her fingers between Hannah's soft slick folds, she felt the proof for herself. Hannah's wetness mingled with the oil, the texture of it lighter, hotter. Abigail sighed as pride swelled inside of her, for it was her touches, her caresses that awakened this pleasure in Hannah. Pleasure Abigail would strengthen so there would be no confusion, no reason for Jameson to doubt how well Hannah felt, how readily her body responded.

Abigail settled her other hand upon Hannah's mound and dipped those fingers between the moist folds. Coating them with Hannah's juices. And then she gripped Hannah's thick lips with the fingers of both hands, and peeled them wide. Knew heat swirled within Hannah for it swirled within herself as well.

Hannah's sighs filled the room. Her muscles tensed. Her breasts and belly quivered as she moaned and trembled against Abigail.

And Abigail sighed with her, moaned with her. Burrowed her fingers further between those hot wet lips, and teased Hannah's swollen nub further out from hiding. Abigail feathered her fingertips over it. Felt its firmness roll beneath her touch. She flicked it and Hannah cried out in pleasure.

Abigail bore the hot damp weight of Hannah's body as it lagged further back against her own. She reveled in it. Thought of how Jameson's body had pressed hers to the wooden table once his seed had reached her womb. His clothing had chafed her naked flesh much like hers must now chafe Hannah's. His body was heavy. Solid. His breaths, like hers, moist and labored. Then, as now, pleasure pulsed within her core in waves of heat. Wetness. Need.

Movement near the hearth drew her attention. Jameson had set another kettle to heat. His steps and the clank of the metal handle on the hook were loud in the quiet room, distracting Abigail from her musings. Hannah stirred as well, and Abigail soothed her. Softened her touch against Hannah, eager to keep Hannah in that place of comfort and pleasure.

Jameson brought Mercy to the wall opposite the hearth. "Clasp your hands at your back," he said, his voice abrupt, though his motions showed no anger. "Stand wide and do not move."

Abigail looked over her shoulder at them. Saw Mercy's hands as Jameson ordered, her legs spread, Jameson securing a shackle to one ankle. He had positioned her where she would be forced to witness all that happened to her sister.

Abigail thought of what was to come and turned to Martha. She stood bound just steps from Mercy. Still clothed, though barely, and shackled to the wall. Her respect for the others was evident from her lowered gaze and whispered prayers. She seemed the most frightened of all. Alone in the world, her children grown, her husband long buried, she remained alone here as well. Waiting her turn. Hearing all that went on. Knowing she too would soon be bared, shaved. Forced to feel not only arousal but release as well. And all for the crime of uttering harsh words against her debtor, now dead.

Jameson came to stand before Hannah, blocking Abigail's view of Martha.

Abigail eased her hands from Hannah's core, wanting Jameson to see Hannah fully.

"Nay," he said, inching closer to them. "Do not stop."

She stroked her fingers over Hannah's bare mound, enjoying the smooth feel of her flesh, like that of a doe, and then she slid them back between the moist folds once again.

Jameson cupped Hannah's chin with his fingers. "You will open your eyes," he said, seeming to study her face.

He sought proof of Hannah's passion, as Abigail had. And though Abigail still felt it on her hands, he would see it for himself in her eyes.

Abigail drew her fingers over the length of Hannah's slick swollen nether lips, feeling, touching every bit of her, wanting her to feel every stroke, every slight tug. Doing all to maintain Hannah's arousal, showing Jameson how her own touch drew Hannah's passion and true responses.

His hot hand covered Abigail's and pressed it firmly to Hannah's mound. Abigail gasped as Hannah moaned, and Jameson moved his hand again, forcing a steady caress against Hannah's nub. Abigail sighed, pressed her legs together to soothe the ache this touch created, for it was as though he pressed their hands against her own mound, forced her to stir her own desires. And then, with a tender grip, he eased Abigail's hand away from Hannah's heat and held it cupped within his own.

A pained whimper of longing came from Hannah. The smallest smile touched Jameson's lips but faded before it settled there. Abigail could not look away, nor could she speak, for waves of pleasure threatened, tensed her body and made each breath heavy in her chest.

With his gaze still on Hannah's face, he urged Abigail's hand back to Hannah's core, shaping Abigail's fingers with his. Cupping them until the heat of Hannah's hot wet passage reached them.

Abigail eagerly obeyed his silent command as he urged her two longest fingers into Hannah. Slowly, slowly, they slid inside, and like a tight moist fist, Hannah's muscles gripped them.

"Open your eyes, Hannah…" Jameson's voice held a whisper of promise, almost beckoning Hannah to feel more, to show more, to sigh and quiver…

He held Abigail's hand still then eased her fingers out as slowly as he had urged them in.

Hannah trembled against Abigail.

"Nay…" he said. "Do not close your eyes…"

Abigail opened hers though he commanded Hannah. And he inched closer, until his lips breathed upon Hannah's ear. "Release is near, is it not?" His tone was low and lulling. A mere breath. "Hannah..." His hold was loose on Abigail's hand. Loose but hot as he guided it up toward Hannah's eyes, showing Hannah how Abigail's fingers glistened by light of the candles.

"'Tis close." Hannah's own voice was breathless. Pleading. Her breasts heaving.

He looked from Hannah to Abigail. "But there is more we must to do," he said, then released Abigail's hand and touched his fingers to her jaw. His probing gaze seeped into her as it had into Hannah, and she had to fight to silence a sigh. He did not look away, but searched Abigail's eyes and stroked her face with his fingertips. The feathery touch from his strong hand making her sway.

"Mind yourself, Abigail," he said, his voice still low and tender. "Do not confuse whose pleasures we are to awaken." He held her gaze a moment more, then turned away.

He knew her secrets. He knew all of their secrets. He touched them, whispered to them, purposely aroused them... And though it was not her place or her time, her body craved yet more. These touches against Hannah, arousing herself as well.

She rubbed her fingers together, further blending Hannah's wetness with the oils still upon them. Never had she touched another woman as she had today. Never had she touched herself but for once, only once, when she had thrust her fingers inside of herself, taking her own virtue. When wanton cries of passion from others in her midst excited her, made her yearn, made her question the longing of her own womb...

Her fingers brought her pleasure then, made her body tremble as though in a fit.

She closed her eyes as need still pulsed beneath her petticoats. Could she touch Hannah further, touch Mercy or Martha without feeling these pleasures herself?

"Bring her." Jameson stood at the table, the large vial in his hand. His gaze steady on her.

Abigail lowered her eyes though she knew not why. He knew well her need. She had no cause to hide it but to tame it, for surely he did the same. She dared a glance toward his breeches. Saw the truth of his desire much as Elizabeth had seen before. Elizabeth had spoken the truth when she said these examinations aroused him. But she knew not the true power of his honor and control.

Abigail drew a breath, deep and slow, then guided Hannah toward the table, urging her to bend over it until her breasts were crushed to the wood. "Reach for the opposite end," she said as Jameson had said to her. "Grip it and do not let go."

With a small shudder, Hannah did as she was told.

Abigail leaned with her, smoothed her hand over Hannah's arm and curled Hannah's fingers to the edge of the table. "You must yield," she said to Hannah. "You must feel that which we do, you must allow it..." She drew her hand back and smoothed it over Hannah's hair, fondling it between her fingers. Brushing it, wisp by wisp, from Hannah's neck, across her back, and settling it to the side.

She feathered her fingertips over Hannah's back, along her spine. Remembering well how those same soft touches from Jameson had aroused her senses.

Each brush of his hand against her, tensed her further. Sent a pulse of heat to her core. No part of her remained untouched, unseen by him. And it would be so for Hannah.

"It will pass quickly," she said in a whisper, "if you are unmarked."

Hannah nodded and Abigail touched a kiss to her shoulder. A small mark there drew her attention and she scratched at it lightly. Hannah stirred from the touch, and Abigail smiled then placed another kiss there, noting a smaller mark, lighter in color, beneath Hannah's ear.

She reached for it as Jameson clasped her hand and drew her to standing. She lifted her eyes to his and noticed how he looked at her, his gaze steady, soft. He breathed deeply, as if smelling her need, letting her know he was aware it lingered still. She looked down to see pleasure still swelled within him as well.

"It is good to feel," she said, looking back at his eyes, "is it not?"

"Only the witch cannot." He turned her hand over and dripped some oil into her palm. "And only the witch cannot be tamed." He held her gaze as firmly as he held her hand. Even as he pressed her hand to Hannah's rump, and had her spread the oil there, he did not look away.

He had said she must contain her arousal yet he aroused her with his touch, with his gaze. And she could not will it away. Like a fire left untended would long smolder, her desire smoldered here this night, not soon to cool.

The languid caresses of their hands on Hannah's generous buttocks, the way their fingers dipped like ribbons into the deep seam between them, danced in time with their breaths, which, too, mingled, hot and moist.

She looked from Jameson's eyes to his lips, pressed together as though desire would sound from them should he part them. She would kiss those lips. Welcome their softness against hers. Had felt it only briefly and craved more. His eyes grew dark and soft and she wondered if, perhaps, his thoughts mirrored hers.

He looked away, turning to Hannah, and a breath, long held, shuddered through Abigail. She would not know his thoughts on this. Not now, for these moments were not for them, but for the accused.

She closed her eyes, let his hand guide hers. Even as he cupped it within his and drew it back, she moved with him. And then he surged their hands forward in a sharp whack against the fleshiest part of Hannah's rump.

Hannah cried out but the spank could not have caused pain for Abigail felt little against her palm. Only warmth and the slightest sting. Jameson drew their hands back again, and landed another spank against Hannah's rump, and another, and another. Quickly they fell against her, harder, hitting the underside of her rump, the side of it, the center. Continuing until Hannah's breaths came hard and wheezing, and Abigail's hand grew hot and tender.

And then he flattened their hands to the spot, now reddened and burning, soothing it with slight and gentle caresses.

"You will widen your stance, Hannah," he said as he dipped his and Abigail's fingers into a small pool of oil on the table.

Realization came to her and she looked up at him with a gasp for she knew not how to touch someone this way.

"You will know when she is ready," he said before she could speak. "But do not fret, Abigail..." He positioned a hand above Hannah's plump cheeks and spread them wide, then brought their oiled fingers to the small withered passage there. "...this will not be as difficult for her..." Together, they caressed that tense and puckered spot, "...as had been for you."

The pressure of Jameson's hand against the spot increased the pressure of Abigail's until Hannah's body grew softer. Easily, the tightness beneath their fingers yielded to their demanding touch. Opened to them as he applied steady pressure and urged Abigail's longest finger and his inside this tight and scalding dark hole.

Hannah did not cry but sighed and arched her back, and Jameson guided their fingers in deeper, the rigid space slowly expanding to allow them in. He withdrew their fingers, his hand expertly working Abigail's, then slid them all the way inside once again, slowly, slowly...

"What do you feel, Hannah?" he asked. "You will tell me."

"As though I might burst..." Her words came out on heaving breaths, "...as a deer from the woods...then stand frozen...unsure where to run."

He withdrew their fingers once more, nearly completely, then plunged them inside with force that drew a wailing cry of need from Hannah.

"Please!" She cried, her body tense, her muscles closing firmly on their fingers. "Where shall I run, oh...tell me."

Jameson held their fingers still, deep inside of Hannah's anus. "Touch her, Abigail," he said. "Reach around her and touch her as you would touch yourself."

Hannah's need burned so hot, Abigail thought she might burst as well. She reached forward, slid her free hand between the thick dripping folds of Hannah's core and found her nub, stiff and swollen with need. She pressed her fingers to it, stroked it gently, firmly, gently again. And then Jameson's free hand gripped her wrist, urged her fingers into Hannah's passage until Abigail impaled her front and back.

Hannah whimpered, trembled as though racked by fits. Abigail used her thumb to find Hannah's nub once more, crying out when Hannah did, feeling passion tighten Hannah's passages, gripping Abigail's fingers as she thrust them into her core and held them still with Jameson's from behind. And then Hannah froze, made no sound, no breath. And Abigail feared both she and Hannah might burst with need.

"This moment is for you, Hannah," Jameson said, his voice as tense as Hannah's body. "Go where you wish."

With a scream, Hannah bucked, her body shuddering, her muscles contracting around the fingers wedged so deeply inside of her, alternately drawing them in and pushing them out.

Still Abigail touched her, more gently now, using Hannah's sighs and spasms to guide her until they slowed and tension slipped from her, allowing Jameson to pull their fingers from her heat.

"You may soothe her," he said as he went to the hearth and splashed water from the kettle over his hands.

Abigail slid her fingers from Hannah's core, then lay atop Hannah, her head on Hannah's back, her heart beating in time with Hannah's, her eyes closed, Hannah's lust fulfilled, Abigail's need still raging.

"Wash the oils from yourself, Abigail," Jameson said, "then start again, with Mercy."

Abigail opened her eyes when he fell silent. He stood at the hearth, his back to her. His body stiff. Still. His hands in front of him where she could not see. And then a noisy breath hissed from him and she knew, without seeing, how he struggled against his own need. She closed her eyes again, let a small smile dance upon her lips, taking comfort in knowing they shared this blissful pain.

"I will tend Martha," he said finally, then turned from the hearth and questioned Martha as he had questioned all of the accused. "Why are you here this night, Martha?"

A silent moment passed.

"Martha..." He all but whispered her name as he strode toward her.

"Please." She whispered as well. "I am an old woman." Fear and shame colored Martha's tone. The same fear and shame Abigail had felt.

She wished to comfort Martha, to be the one to examine her. She shifted, looked where they stood, saw Jameson slowly approach Martha while Mercy looked on, seeming unconcerned that she stood naked and spread before all of them.

"You are not so old, Goody Farrington," Jameson said to Martha, "that you cannot recall the reason you are here." He reached her and she looked up at him, slowly shaking her head then tipping it back, as he drew closer still.

He lifted a hand, touched the back of his fingers to her face, smoothed them down along her cheek. "Why are you here, Martha? I will hear the words."

The grinding creak of hinges sounded in the hall. Then boot steps, heavy. Quick. Jameson turned toward the door as the boot steps neared it.

Abigail, stood, tried to block the view of Hannah lest someone burst through the door and see her, but she could do naught to block Mercy.

Jameson's stride devoured the distance to the door. He set his palm high and flat to it as loud harsh pounding came from the other side.

"Governor!" It was the watchman. "Governor? You are needed in the yard."

Elizabeth. "No." Abigail took a step toward Jameson, could move herself no further when the watchman spoke again.

"It is most urgent."

The passion roiling through Abigail turned to terror, racing her heart the same, tightening her chest, taking her breath. "Jameson... Good Sir... please..."

He turned toward her but did not meet her gaze. "Shackle them until my return," he said, then opened the door just enough to pass through and closed it firmly behind him.

Chapter Eight

Elizabeth no longer felt the cold air against her naked flesh. She felt only the lingering tingle from hands that had touched her, hands that had pinched, struck and probed. The very core of her felt stretched and opened for all, as if the watchman's fingers still spread her and the phallus still plunged into her.

Her shoulders ached. The shackles still held her arms overhead. The watchman had made them tight enough to prevent release, loose enough to prevent pain. He was a considerate man.

Her breaths came slow as if she slept, for she had not the strength to draw deeply, yet she lifted her head, tried to focus her gaze and search for him. Only a sea of torches and capes lay before her, the faces of all had turned toward the manor, their voices rising with hatred and desire for blood. Her blood.

She would not think it. She would think only of the watchman's mercy. He vowed no harm would come to her, that she would be safe with him near.

Still in search of him, her gaze fell over the crowd once more.

A sudden loud rumble came from them, and she sought the cause. Governor Foster came from the manor and stood atop its stairs. Her watchman stood beside him, shoulder to shoulder, speaking. He turned to where she stood bound. Descended the stairs, headed toward her. He would rescue her. Save her from the madness.

He reached her in silence and though she looked to him as he had commanded, he did not look to her.

"Pray," she said, her voice soft but sure. "What will happen to me?"

He released the shackles and her arms dropped to her sides. They throbbed, tingled.

He bound her hands behind her again, and led her toward the manor, the crowd parting as they passed.

She looked into their accusing eyes. Would not be humbled even now, naked and stained by their vile touches. She had felt every slap of their hands, every pinch. She felt her nether lips spread, her virtue breeched by fingers and phallus. Even from behind she had been tested, fingers inserted deep inside of her, pumping to a rhythm she could not escape. She had felt the humiliation, the heat. They knew. They saw. They heard and they felt her responses. Since a witch could not feel, they could not condemn her. Except by wicked lies to the heavens.

She stumbled as she climbed the manor stairs but the watchman held her, urged her forward without words until she stood a step below the governor.

"You will not look away from me."

Slowly she raised her eyes and looked into the governor's angry gaze.

"You knew yourself marked. That is why you refused my examination."

Her body, her eyes, felt heavy. "I am not marked."

"They have examined you," he said, indicating the crowd. "They say you bear the mark."

"They are mistaken."

He looked to the watchman beside her but she kept her gaze on him.

"Where is this mark?" he asked.

The watchman released his hold on her bound wrists and reached for her leg.

"Nay! You will not touch her. You will tell me."

The watchman dropped his hand. "It is near her womanhood. To her left."

The governor nodded. "Cut her loose so she may show me the mark," he said and the watchman released her bound wrists.

She hesitated, unsure what he sought.

He pointed to a spot beside him on the right. "You will place your foot here," he said, forcing her to set one leg higher, opening herself to him.

He took a slight step closer to her, spoke for all to hear. "Spread yourself for me."

His gaze held steady on hers and though he did not speak further she knew he meant to shame her, to have her give herself to him now though she had refused before. Was it not enough to be naked before all? To stand with her legs wide? He could see what he wanted; she did not need to expose herself more.

"You dawdle? Have you no care for those within the manor? Those so eager to prove their innocence they willingly do as asked?"

"What is asked," she said, "conflicts with what is right."

"Innocents freely submit, while witches hide behind selfish pride."

"Whether prideful or submissive, innocents are oft maligned."

"Do you refuse?"

"Nay." She would neither give him cause to force her nor cower before him. "I will prove my innocence."

With her gaze on his, she reached between her legs and pulled her thigh taut, holding herself wide even as he slowly bent before her, his moist breath heating her core. And then his fingers probed a spot on her thigh. Her body felt numb. From cold. From the cruel pinches. From this humiliation. She would not let him see how this touch above all shamed her.

She kept her gaze on him, her eyes lowered as he leaned yet closer, until the hair on his head tangled with the hair of her mons.

"You smell of lust," he said, then rose to his feet. "Their touches aroused you?" He stood so near, she felt the warmth of his body.

She would not provide the answer he sought, would not add to his vulgar thoughts.

"She did respond," the watchman said. "With sighs and quivers."

With sudden forcefulness, the governor cupped his hand to her core, shocking her with its bold searing heat. Her breath caught, her belly tightened. She trembled but did not pull away, did not look away. Deftly, his fingers spread her, smoothed to and fro against the wetness there.

She swallowed her cry of surprise, unwilling to let him see how such touches heated her. And then he slid a finger deep inside of her, pulsed it within. A horrified whimper escaped her tight lips, for despite her humiliation, it aroused her.

A grimace contorted his mouth, his eyes turned hard, and though his solid finger within her teased and pleasured, she kept her gaze on his, fearful and unsure what thoughts he had. And then he withdrew his hand from her and ordered the watchman to bind her wrists again.

"You should have submitted to me, Elizabeth. I would have spared you this shame."

She pressed her legs together, trying in vain to wipe the feel of his hand from her. "You have done the same." She could not keep the venom from her voice. "Your touch is meant to shame and to —"

The watchman tugged the ropes tight, hurting her, silencing her. "There was no mark until the end," he said.

The governor drew himself taller. "I will hear your thoughts."

"I bound her, spread, before all and did not see it." He glanced at the crowd then back to the governor. "I fear it was made by one of them."

Thankful for the watchman's words, she remained silent, awaited the governor's response, breath held, as his gaze traveled over her. He would know the watchman spoke only truth. She was not marked until they had touched her. Surely the mark was theirs. The governor could spare her. He could declare her unmarked.

He touched her then, passing his fingers over her lips, his fingertips brushing beneath her nose, forcing her to inhale the thick musty aroma of her own decadent juices.

"Your scent is heady upon my hand," he said, lightly dragging his fingertips down past her lips, over her chin, her neck and to the sensitive flesh between her breasts. "If you had submitted to me, your scent would have filled my chamber, and there would be no questions, no doubt. None of your foolish pride." His hot hand covered her breast, gently squeezed, caressed.

She shuddered as much from his touch as from his words.

He leaned closer to her, spoke softly in her ear. "I would have taken time to arouse you so pride would no longer betray you." The whisper of his breath bathed her neck in moist heat. "I would have touched you, Elizabeth. Warmed you. Awakened the heat within you until you screamed from the freedom and the pleasure of it."

He clasped her nipple between two fingers, held it tightly making it throb. "And I would have known the truth of your responses." He loosened his hold, then clasped tight again and it felt as if his fingers had buried into her wetness once more. "Instead you chose this…" He pulled away. She felt cold, shivered as he touched his hands to her shoulders and turned her toward the crowd. "Look at them, Elizabeth."

She could not keep from trembling. She was all they feared, all they loathed. "But I am not marked."

"They believe you are," he said. "And if it is proven, they will not have your crime go unpunished."

She dared look up at him as he looked out over the crowd, his brow furrowed as if he had fallen deep into thought. When his gaze met hers, she feared the coldness of it and quickly humbled herself before he could speak, hoping he might spare her the worst fate of all.

"Pride does not portend guilt." The words trembled as they broke past her lips. "I felt their touch." She felt shame flame her face. "And yours."

He waved a hand, dismissing her. "Take her into the forest," he said loudly, without another glance her way. "Bind her to the old oak until sunrise."

The crowd came to life, shouting and waving their fists and their torches. Cheering the removal of a witch from their sights.

"No!" She struggled in the watchman's grip as the governor turned away. "I am unmarked!"

He entered the manor and shut the door, leaving her to beg the watchman for mercy.

"You know this to be wrong."

He took her down the stairs, through the crowd.

"Release me!" She struggled in his grasp but it was no use. "I am unmarked!"

"Cease!" He pushed her ahead of him and she stumbled to her knees. He caught her before she fell flat, and whispered in her ear. "They are sure of what they saw." He helped her to her feet and walked her forward. "They would have their village cleansed of evil."

"I am not evil. I am not marked."

"They will not be convinced."

He took her beyond the gates, beyond the platform. Her body trembled as they reached the path she had been forced to take at midnight, when she and the others were led from the forest to town to be displayed for all.

She could not go back, could not let him leave her there, naked, bound and alone. Open to the cold, the animals, and fate.

Dread made her weak and unsteady as they stepped into the darkness. The crunch of leaves, branches, and cold earth muted the shouts from the crowd. The thick forest blocked all light from the moon and torches. She had wished for the moon to move swiftly. Now she prayed for it to remain high in the sky, for sunrise would not bring freedom. It would bring punishment.

The oak came into view as a single torch beside it lit the way. He bound her as she had been bound at twilight – the bark sticking her back, her limbs open wide, as if in offering to familiars who might choose to suckle. But there would be no familiars. She was not a servant of the beast.

"I am not marked." She closed her eyes, felt the heat of her own tears on her face.

"You weep." The watchman touched her tears, rubbed them between his fingers.

"I am frightened."

"Were you not frightened before?"

"You said they would not harm me."

He cupped his hand to her cheek, stroked it with his thumb. "I could only spare you their worst abuse. I cannot spare you the governor's decree."

"But I am unmarked," she said. "He knows this to be true." She tipped her head into his hand, welcoming the gentleness of his touch. "You know it, too."

He dropped his hand and she feared he would leave her. The terror of that filled her for it would be hours before he would come back for her. And when he did, it could be to bring her to the gallows.

"The mark is theirs," she said, unable to stop from spilling more tears. "Please... might I know your name?"

"I am Giles."

"Please, Giles...do not leave me to this fate."

He touched the mark on her thigh. Smoothed his hand over it in a gentle caress that showed a battle brewed within him. The tenderness of his touch comforted her, confused her. Proved to her own mind that she was unmarked, for his touch would not warm her as it did if she could not feel it. She wanted more of it. Would take what he would give if only to prove, to him as well, that she, unlike the witch, felt as much the lightest flutter against her flesh as the cruelest probe.

"Test me yourself." She trembled at her own whispered words but knew no other way. He lifted his gaze to hers and she saw the unspoken question there.

"I submit. To you," she said. "I wish to prove my innocence. Test me and I will."

"It is not my place to examine you." Even as he said the words, he drew closer to her.

"You have shown me great tenderness and concern. You will be merciful even in this. Please."

"I cannot proclaim you guilty or innocent. That is only for the governor —"

"He asked your thoughts. He will believe you."

His eyes were gentle. His body solid and strong. He could do much harm to her if he so desired. But how much harm awaited her now, bound and at the governor's mercy?

"It is my body," she said. "I do not give it freely." She tensed in both relief and fear as he touched his hands to her waist. "I do so now to save my life."

He dropped his hands and turned away in silence.

The Accused

She stared after him, fear silencing her as he grabbed the lone torch and retreated down the path, plunging her into the shadow of night.

Chapter Nine

Jameson fell back against the manor doors, letting the heavy wood mute the angry cries and riotous shouts from the yard. If not for the venom in the voices of the crowd, the fury and fear in their eyes, he would not have sent Elizabeth to the forest. But they would accept no less, not while in such a frenzied state.

"Good Sir?"

He tipped his head back until it, too, touched the door, his eyes lifted to the ceiling, his vision clouded by despair for having failed to erode her defenses.

"Is it Elizabeth? Good Sir? Jameson..."

Abigail's hand was hot against his, his body still chilled from the outside air, still cold from the heartless command he had been compelled to give. "She is prideful."

"Pride is not witchcraft."

He rested his eyes for a brief moment, saw the image of Elizabeth. Stubborn yet fearful. Naked and humbled. Too late.

"I would seek to prove innocence," he said. "I would be diligent in my quest. They..." He pushed off the door, held a hand toward it, as if to the crowd as they shouted still. "They seek guilt. They see it in their hearts before they think it, before they prove it and then 'tis there. Everywhere they look."

"They...deem her marked?"

"Aye."

"Jameson...no...you know she is not."

He looked at Abigail then, saw the pleading in her wide blue eyes. The hope, the innocent belief in fairness and truth. "I know naught," he said, "save her pride and willfulness."

"You can help her. You can tell them —"

He slammed the side of his fist to the door yet felt no relief from the gesture. They would hang her themselves if he did not send her to the forest. "She has chosen her fate."

There were others to tend. He stormed down the hall toward his antechamber, snatched the door handle. Scoffed when Abigail thrust her slight frame between him and the door, as if to block his entry. He dropped his hand.

"Please..." Abigail did not blink, but searched his eyes with hers. "You must."

Nothing could be done. The crowd would have Elizabeth suffer the elements until she confessed. Or until dawn when judgment would be meted. "Time does not wait, Abigail. You will step aside."

"I cannot." She straightened. Squared her slender shoulders. "Your anger will frighten the others." She looked at him, expectant, but he had no response. "You fear, too, for Elizabeth," she said. "That fear, your fear and your anger, will grip the others and alter their true responses."

"You assume much."

"I do not assume," she said, then softened her stance. "I know. I saw your anger when you thought me marked. I felt your anger. I feared for my life and my soul. And then you calmed and saw truth. I beg you now, Jameson." She lifted her hands, flattened her palms to his chest. "Calm."

He had treated her poorly when he examined her. Had believed her most deceitful, hiding the mark from him when in fact the mark he saw upon her breast had been but a smudge as she had declared, nothing more. He would have punished her cruelly for that deception...

He turned away from her pleading eyes, her gentle touch, and went to the stairs, resting his forearms on the rail. He would calm. The women within his chamber were not Elizabeth. They had not refused. They had chosen to submit and trusted him to show mercy, fairness. Patience.

She stood beside him again. Laid her hands on his arm. He liked the feel of them there and covered them with one of his, welcoming her tenderness, her compassion.

"If you are that afraid for Elizabeth," she said, "perhaps you might examine her for all to see. If she is truly marked—"

A harsh sound of dismissal he did not intend to make came from his throat. "Elizabeth…" he shook his head, "…did not resist for fear of being found marked. She hid for pride."

"Then…" Her hands kneaded his arm. "…you will prove she is unmarked, and they will see."

"She would not submit." He pushed off the rail, paced the space as she stood back.

"'Tis her life now," she said. "She would submit. I assure you."

He faced her, saw how deeply she believed her words. "You might seek to compromise yourself, Abigail, but Elizabeth would not. She is too proud. And that pride will bring her hanging."

"I do not compromise myself, Good Sir," she said with a petulant lift of her chin. "Never more, yet thrice here this night."

He had not meant to insult but to state truth, yet he allowed her to speak.

"Once, out there, in the yard," she said, "when I permitted those filthy hands to touch me." She pointed to his chamber. "A second time, in there, with you, as you bade me disrobe and bend over, presenting myself so you might do your bidding. And again, when you deemed me marked and I, of my own accord, presented proof of my innocence, there, naked, spread and wetted." She drew closer to him with each word. "And you took that proof, did you not, Jameson? You touched it with your hands, your fingers."

He remained where he was, crossed his arms over his chest as she closed the space between them.

Remembering well the moments of which she spoke for she had faced them with bravery, had struggled with her shame and budding passions much as her passions had caused a struggle within him.

"You smelled it as it filled the room," she said, her voice growing softer, less heated. "Felt it as it aroused you, as it urged you to seek release and offer release to me as well." She stood a mere breath from him, her hands on his arms. "I accepted it, then, Jameson. To prove my innocence... as Rebecca accepted it. As Hannah. As would Elizabeth now if you ask her. As I would again now... for you see..." Her voice grew softer still, her gaze held his. "I do not compromise myself but offer that which you seek...for I seek it as well...for reasons beyond fear..."

He lowered his hands to her waist. "I fear you know well your words, Abigail, but not well their meaning." He ached to tear the dress from her body, to touch her flesh as he had before...

He dropped his hands from her. "You would be wise to think before you next speak so boldly."

"I know well my meaning, Good Sir." She did not move but to press her hot hands to his chest. "I offer myself now as a wedge between your anger and the women inside." Her body pressed to his, her softness further rousing his hardening desire, challenging his control. "I offer myself now," she said, "as a reminder that guilt and innocence may not always be as they seem...and I offer myself now for I want, and I need...as do you."

He could take no more, could resist no more. He snatched her upper arms, pushed her across the hall to the far wall, hitting her back to it, pressing her there. And then he ravaged her mouth with his, tasting her, devouring her, crushing her beneath his straining need until she whimpered.

He drew back. "This is what you seek, Abigail?" He spun her around to face the wall and leaned in hard against her, his erection firm against her rump. "This?"

"I have felt your strength," she said, breathless and trembling, "and seek more of it."

He would give her all she sought, all he had. He snatched her skirts with one hand and drew them to her hips then reached between her silken thighs and skimmed two fingers through her slit. She was slick and ready, as though still drenched in oils. He thrust his fingers deep inside of her and her harsh cry was one of lust, of surprise, of want. He withdrew his fingers and thrust them inside of her again, his breaths heaving in time with hers.

His eager cock strained against his breeches and he pulled his fingers from her, freed himself. Then, with an arm wrapped around her waist, he yanked her hips back toward his and plunged his throbbing cock into her. He withdrew then plunged back in, hearing her sighs and his own rasping breaths. He pressed against her, drove deeper, seeking to fill her yet further, though he had naught left to give for she had taken all of him, every inch to the hilt.

He nearly withdrew then plunged inside again and again and again. Not stopping, not slowing.

Their breaths came hard and harsh, mating as their bodies mated. At once taking and giving, both urgent and wet. And his blood surged, tightened his sac as though all his seed heaved upward, flooding his cock, making it swell yet further. Pleasuring him, torturing him. And still he thrust into her. She took him in deep each time, held him within, gripped him tight, made each withdrawal a challenge to his control.

He sought her lips, those luscious lips that spoke bold lustful words. And when he found them, he pressed his against them, sunk his tongue between them as they opened for him. Explored, tangled it with hers, withdrew and plunged in again, taking her mouth as his cock took her quim, their scents mingling, their moans echoing in the hall, making their mating calls sound like a thousand more. And still his blood surged, filling his cock until he could stand no more.

He broke the kiss. "Abigail."

Her breaths rasped from her throat. Her quim convulsed around him.

"Touch yourself as you please." He fumbled to lift the front of her skirts, then covered her hand with his and pressed it to her slit. Her fingertips, stiff and straight, grazed his cock as it slid in and out of her from behind. Faster, harder. "Now. Abigail. Now."

Her fingers flexed and stretched beneath his as they frantically danced over her wet swollen core. Faster and faster she went, and then she stilled, seemed not to breathe, and he withdrew completely, then surged forward, slamming against her, filling her again, his swollen head pressed to her womb, his body tensing, his blood and seed rising, higher, higher.

She moaned, long and low, and her body gripped tighter to him, sent his senses into blinding darkness until his seed burst from him in wave after wave of agonizing pleasure, spilling into her, filling her, mingling with her juices, pulsing with her convulsions. His heaving breaths echoed by hers. His heart pounding against her back, his fingers, now laced with hers, gently stroking her still-swollen lips, bared as they were and bald. Sticky and wet, dripping with her lust and his seed.

He rested fully against her then, reveling in the ebbing flow of her release until it ceased. He eased himself from her heat, felt the coolness of the air against his retreating cock, and set it away, securing his breeches and letting her skirts fall to their length. She remained against the wall, her hands flat to it beside her face, her cheek pressed there, her eyes closed, her mouth opened, inviting him to sip from her lips once more in a light, lingering touch. He pressed against her softness, took that sip. And another.

Sated. Drained. Soothed. He set his forearms on the wall above her, resting there behind her, against her.

Her eyes fluttered open. "I have decried your strength, Good Sir," she said with a small smile. "For I fear, without this wall to brace me, I am unable to stand."

A short laugh escaped him, for he shared that same fear. He eased his weight from her then turned her to face him. She leaned back against the wall and he cupped her face in his hands.

"You have bewitched me, Abigail." He smoothed his hands back over her hair, tilting her head up as he did.

His smile formed but felt heavy and he let it fall, thinking of the women who still waited, of Elizabeth now bound and alone in the dark forest.

"These examinations..." He shook his head, thought of all he had performed. "I do not believe so many to be marked." He tipped his head forward, touched his forehead to hers. He thought to confess to her what he confessed to no one save Giles, but he dared not. "I would end this madness," he said simply, "had I the power to do so." He closed his eyes, knew in his heart he would rather a witch go free than an innocent be hanged.

Her fingers, delicate and light, brushed his cheek. "You think of Elizabeth."

"Aye." He lifted his head from hers. "But I do not feel anger as I felt before." He touched her as she touched him, a light brush of his fingertips against her cheek. Then he tipped his head and reached in for a small kiss. Her lips clung to his, seemed to pull him to her and he lingered there, taking, giving, wanting. He ended the kiss then drew a full breath. "The others await."

He left her soft warmth completely, reached for the door to his antechamber then turned back when she did not move.

"Can you stand freely?" He smiled when she did.

"Aye," she said, "but I fear I may be unable to walk."

C380

Abigail entered the chamber behind Jameson. Her body still weak and trembling from the power of his touches, her core beneath her petticoats still wet from his seed and her juices.

She glanced at the others, Mercy and Hannah naked and bound, Martha still clothed. Would they know? Had they heard? Could they smell the scent of arousal upon her body?

She straightened her back, smoothed her hands over her skirts. It would not matter. It would neither affect their innocence nor their guilt. She looked at Martha. She was a pious woman near sixty, so ashamed she dared not look upon the others even as they stood naked beside her. Abigail feared for her and wished to spare her the indignities yet to come.

The clank of metal drew Abigail's attention to Jameson. He stood at the hearth, firelight lining his solid form from behind. His breadth and strength magnified as he lifted the heavy water-filled kettle from its hook with ease then settled it on the floor beside the hearth.

He went to her then. "You will release Mercy and Martha," he said, handing her the key to their shackles.

She looked at Mercy, saw her gaze steady and bold on Jameson. A hunger shining there that should not be. But Jameson seemed not to notice as he went to the chest and knelt before it, his broad back and powerful legs pulling taut the fabric of his doublet and breeches, exposing for all his powerful form.

She thought of his strength and how he had touched her just moments before. His hands, rough. Forceful. Claiming her as she yielded. Arousing her...making her crave. She thought of his kiss, demanding one moment, tender the next. And she ached for him still, though her attention should be as his. Focused on the next examination.

She released Mercy's shackles. The heavy irons clanked loudly in the otherwise silent room as she dropped them to the floor. And then she released Martha. But Hannah remained.

"Good Sir?"

He closed the chest and strode to the table, a large tow cloth pouch in his hands. She started to follow, then stopped as he set the pouch on the table. The heavy clunk of irons within it assailed her, reminded her of the tools he had used on her, the biting pain of iron clamps on her nipples, the relentless pressure of the stone phallus he bade her body accept, and the spar he had oiled and wedged, slowly, deeply inside of her rump until she feared she be might split in two.

He faced her then, expectant, but her words scrambled on her tongue, her mind dizzy from memories of her body's responses, and concerned for those still to be examined.

"You will bring Martha to me, now," he said, and she feared more for Martha, wished he, with his harsh examination tools, would examine Mercy instead. And yet...she did not wish to see Mercy writhe beneath his touch...

She turned, grasped Martha's cold hand, squeezed it gently and led her to Jameson's side. "Good Sir..." she began as he touched a palm to Martha's face, his fingers in her hair, combing it back gently. The gesture appearing more intimate than his fondling of the others.

"Hannah..." Abigail continued, distracted. "Must she remain so? She has been declared unmarked. Perhaps –"

"She will remain," he said, then looked past Martha to Hannah. "You may take your ease."

Hannah glanced at her twin, at Mercy, who gave her a nod, and then Hannah lowered herself to the floor, sitting as decorously as her nakedness would allow.

"You will examine Mercy," Jameson said, his attention shifting from Mercy back to Martha. "I will now hear your answer. Why are you here this night?"

"I spoke in anger," she said. "That is all."

"You show no sorrow for the pain of your words."

"My words are mere sounds, they cannot..." Her voice quivered as he took a step yet closer to her and he slid his other hand through her hair to cradle her head, his thumbs gently brushing her face. "My words cannot..."

"Tell me," he said softly.

"They cannot cause harm," she said, "for I am not a witch."

He smoothed his hands downward, cupped her shoulders, traced his palms along the length of her arms. And she sighed. Trembled. Abigail trembled as well, all but feeling his hands on her flesh, warm, gentle. Though this time, his caresses were not without intent. He sought a rough patch. A deadened spot. A mark. Martha, in her quest to remain pious and honorable, would resist, for she did not yet know that honor here, within these walls, meant abandon.

"If it be your wish to prove it so, I will hear the words."

Abigail held her breath, wished for Jameson's patience to last.

"If you are not a witch," he said in that low alluring tone, "then you seek to prove yourself unmarked, do you not?"

Martha sighed. Closed her eyes, then opened them quickly. "Aye."

"Proof requires much." His hands went to her waist, then slid lower to sit upon her hips. "What permissions do you grant me this night?"

The air went still. Thick. Abigail reached for Martha, her intent to encourage, then withdrew as Martha relented. "All," she said, "for I fear I must."

The smallest flicker of relief softened Jameson's gaze and Abigail smiled, aware how thoughts of Elizabeth burdened his mind, and how he feared others might choose the same fate as she.

Herself relieved, she went to Mercy. Martha had naught to fear. Jameson would be gentle.

"Are you well, Mercy?" Abigail asked, recalling the blood on Jameson's blade as he shaved her.

"I am," Mercy said, her voice clear, her eyes on Jameson, "for he has declared my sister unmarked."

Abigail turned Mercy toward the light of the candle on the wall, setting Mercy's back to Jameson and Martha. "I hope to prove the same for you," Abigail said, "as Governor Foster has proved for Hannah." She touched Mercy the same as Jameson would have, caressing her arms, searching her flesh, watching her responses, certain they would be true, for though lust itself had condemned her, it could now save her.

She cupped a hand to Mercy's cheek. Stroked her fingertips over Mercy's neck, then grazed them lower, to the outer curve of Mercy's breasts, aware her hand was not as Jameson's. Not as strong, sure or warm. But Mercy craved touches both forceful and tender. She had admitted so and was punished, though her time in the pillory for such passionate crimes did naught to subdue her desires. And so she was here, for lustful tendencies such as those she displayed could only be those of the witch.

"You will disrobe." Jameson's order to Martha stalled Abigail's hands at Mercy's waist. His tone, though gentle, left no question. No room for hesitation. Abigail closed her eyes. Waited, hoped Martha would be quick to obey.

"You will look at me," Jameson said, and though he spoke to Martha, Abigail opened her eyes and did as he ordered. His gaze held a gentle determination. The line of his lips, though thin, was soft. He gave Martha a small nod. Did not smile. "That is good," he said then stood back, clearly waiting for her to disrobe. "No. Do not close your eyes."

"When an old woman stands bare," she said softly, "all of nature weeps. It is a sight I cannot bear."

As the words faded, he reached for her, eased her torn shift from her shoulders and slowly peeled it down the length of her arms. Martha's heavy breaths, Abigail's as well, pulsed within the room. Jameson did not speak, did not hesitate yet did not rush as he pulled her shift past Martha's wrists and fingers to let it hang freely, baring her full to the waist. And then he tugged loose the bow at Martha's waist. She released a small cry.

He did not acknowledge it but allowed her petticoat to slip past her hips, taking her shift with it, down her legs and to the floor, his hands following until they swept down from her waist, following every dip and swell of her body to her knees, then back up again. He stood back then, his gaze dipping low then rising slowly up to her face.

"I assure you, Goody Farrington," he said, "at this sight, nature does not weep."

Abigail swallowed a sigh, pleased Martha stood beneath Jameson's tender gaze and knowing hands. He did not bind Martha, spread, to the table but shifted her until she stood by light of the hearth, her legs wide, her hands clasped at her back.

"The blade is most sharp," he said as he sat upon the stool before her, pressing a dampened cloth to her core. "You will remain still."

Abigail watched his tender ministering a moment longer then turned back to Mercy, smoothing her palms over the silken flesh of Mercy's full thighs. Her hips. No mark of an unnatural form marred her lovely flesh. No teat protruded. Abigail skimmed her hands higher, noted a small darkened spot upon Mercy's shoulder. The same as upon Hannah. Tested and natural. But there was another. One not examined.

Gently, Abigail brushed Mercy's hair to the side, exposing her neck. There, in the same spot and form as on her sister, lay a grayish mark, pale in the center, not fully circular... But of course they would bare similar marks. They were twins. It would be from birth, like their eyes, their hair, the wide swell of their hips. This could not be otherwise for surely the beast would not mark them the same.

She glanced at Jameson, not willing to draw his attention should this mark be not worthy of concern. Ever so gently, she brushed Mercy's hair from the other side, letting it fall at Mercy's back, then stroked her own fingers over Mercy's neck and shoulder, seeing nothing there as on the opposite side.

Then, with her fingernail, she scraped the mark, but at that moment, it was Martha, not Mercy who gasped.

"That is good, Martha." Jameson still sat before her, a hand cupped to her freshly shaved core, his fingers buried deeply between Martha's nether lips. Though Abigail could not see where they touched, it was clear from the quiver of Martha's belly, the tension of her mouth, her full breaths, that his long thick fingers impaled her, testing her responses as he had tested Abigail and the others.

"You wish to resist," he said to Martha. "Yet your body yields."

"Forgive," she said, shame constricting her voice.

"No." He stood with his body so close to Martha she would feel the heat of him. The power. Her body would betray her mind as Abigail's body had betrayed hers. But unlike Martha, Abigail had relented, no longer fighting the pleasure of Jameson's touch.

"I seek more from you, Martha. All you have." His tone was like a warm swirl of smoke from the hearth; it swept through the room. To Abigail it was as though he spoke to her. Caressed her. Embraced her. Mercy and Hannah, too, watched him. Their own breaths hitching as he stood yet closer to Martha, adjusting his hand against her core, making her gasp again, her eyes pleading with his. The tendons in his forearm flexed with each clear thrust of his fingers inside her.

"Do not deny what your body craves," he said, softly, "for it is only in your pleasure where innocence shall be found." He withdrew his hand then, and the first signs of abandon flushed pink upon Martha's face.

Abigail did the same to Mercy, brushing her hand over the soft slight swell of Mercy's belly, then smoothing her fingers over Mercy's shaved core, her lips smooth, lush and damp. Abigail eased a finger into Mercy's wet heat.

Though as Martha sighed and whimpered, Mercy remained silent. As Martha stood tense and flushed, Mercy remained calm, removed. Her gazed steady on Abigail's. Mercy's experience was great and varied. Abigail's was limited to her awakenings this night. She glanced at Martha. Had feared it would be her knowledge of passion that would limit her responses. Yet it was Mercy's. Perhaps Jameson's hand was the better choice. She glanced at him, then clenched her eyes, not wanting to imagine his hands so intimately upon Mercy. His fingers slick from her wetness, his senses filled by her sighs, her scent.

No. She would arouse Mercy. Do all Jameson would do and bring her pleasure. For if the haze of need did not reach Mercy's eyes, Jameson would seek it himself, disappointed in both Abigail's attempts and Mercy's responses.

Abigail withdrew her finger from Mercy's core, then slid it back inside, listening for some sign, feeling for even the smallest shiver of need. She pulsed her finger against the soft wet wall of Mercy's quim, noted the slickness and scent of Mercy's heat. Slight, but there.

She needed more. As much as she could draw, for Jameson, with one glance, would know if Mercy's passions were true. Concern for Mercy warred with the pain Jameson's touches against her would bring to Abigail's heart. He would seek proof of the lust for which Mercy was known. Insatiable desire, it were told, that lasted long and rendered most men incapable.

She cupped her free hand to Mercy's full rump, held her firmly then added another finger to her core, the two slipping easily into Mercy's wetness. Her belly tensed.

A slight quiver only, but Abigail felt small relief, and pressed her fingers more deeply within, withdrawing only to insert yet another, not wishing to harm but to draw sighs genuine and unrestrained.

Martha's whimper distracted them all. Abigail stilled, one hand tight on Mercy's rump, the fingers of the other piercing her wet core, fully planted within until they could thrust no further.

Jameson stood beside Martha, the crop in his hand, its leather tip beneath her chin. He drew it down her body, between her breasts, then tapped it back and forth to each, once, twice, three times. Making them sway, coloring them pink. And then he struck her nipples, first one then the other. Martha cried out as Mercy's quim tightened on Abigail's fingers, her own core heating, throbbing with every beat of her quickening heart.

Abigail wished not to feel pleasure from Martha's pain. But Martha would feel pleasure, too, for that was Jameson's wish. A multitude of sensations, a mix of emotions. Desire. Shame. Awareness. And he observed each, sought each. Demanded them. Gauging sighs, cries, even quivering flesh and dripping need. Feeling it, inhaling it. Satisfying it.

A small sound, like a laugh, came from Mercy. Abigail opened her eyes, not realizing she had closed them.

Mercy smiled as she studied Abigail, though Abigail did not understand why.

"You are too quick to respond," Mercy said, her voice hushed, her head dipped toward Abigail's. "There is but little pleasure when need rises so soon."

"I seek not my own pleasure, Mercy, but your surrender, so you might be found unmarked."

Mercy's smile grew then slowly faded. Her gaze unwavering as it held Abigail's. Her stance bold as she shifted, pushed her hips more fully against Abigail's hand, her own hands hot as they circled Abigail's waist. Smoothed upward, to graze her breasts, sending sharp tingles through to Abigail's core.

Mercy leaned closer. Whispered softer, her voice barely audible over the slap of leather against flesh. "Do not drip for him, Abigail," she said, "His touches this night are not for you alone but for us. All of us."

Abigail withdrew her fingers from Mercy, pushed her away, breathed through the unexpected, unwanted pleasure of her caress, and looked past her to Jameson.

His back to her, he set the crop upon the mantle. Abigail had but to take it and use it on Mercy, though it be not her flesh but her caustic tongue which deserved a lashing.

She could not. Despite Mercy's wicked words and wayward hands, Abigail could not strike her, or anyone. She could not cause pain.

Instead, she gripped Mercy's arm and brought her to the table, pressed her down until she lay with her breasts flattened against the wood, somewhat surprised Mercy did not resist. And then she dripped the oils over Mercy's rump and into the deep crease between her plump cheeks. She would see that Mercy's passions dripped freely, too. That her need grew as great as the others', both for her insolence and for her…

Abigail shook her head. Angered with herself for seeking to punish Mercy with pleasure, for thinking to force it from her despite her submission. Hurting her when gentle persuasion would suffice.

But Mercy was more knowing than Abigail could ever be. Like Martha, her passions had been tasted, tested, well before this night. Though unlike Martha, who succumbed to the practiced touch of Jameson's strong hands, Mercy had only Abigail, herself only just aware what pleasures could be had.

She poured a bit of the oil onto the table, blinking back tears. She was asked only to arouse Mercy and she failed. That failure could unleash Jameson's wrath against Mercy, or his most patient and probing touches. Both pained her deeply.

She dipped her fingers into the oil, coating them as Jameson had. But even in this she was ill-prepared, for she had not performed this test without his assistance.

Swallowing her sadness, she closed her eyes then drew a breath and calmed. "Good sir?" She turned to see Jameson watching her, his gaze as heated and probing as his touch.

He turned back to Martha. "Widen your stance," he said, his hand on her thigh, pressing. "Wider. Now lift your eyes to mine, Martha, do not look away."

Slowly she raised her eyes to his, though the effort seemed great. Her breasts hung low and free, glistening from the oils he had spread there. She had suffered few strikes from the crop, yet her nipples puckered and protruded and Abigail knew how they ached to be touched.

"Good," he said softly, "Hold your hands tightly at your back and do not let go."

She nodded, her gaze on his, near pleading, even as he turned for the tools he had set onto the mantle. Abigail now worried for Martha. Would he clamp those thick nipples as he had clamped hers?

The thought of seeing the heavy irons hang from another woman's breasts made her feel the weight of them against her own, as if they still hung there. But the pain of removal... if he had not tended her so well...

He grabbed the stone phallus, large in his grasp, and Martha's breath quivered from her. He turned away, and with only a glance at Mercy's glistening rump, he went to the table and reached for the large vial, carefully, deliberately pouring its oil onto the stone then coating it so until it glistened in the firelight.

"It will fill you," he said, his stride almost lazy as he went to Martha. "And you will hold it within." He cupped her core with his oiled hand, rubbed his fingers over her nether lips, coating them, making her tremble, falter in her wide stance. His voice, a low hum, held a tender patience as he told her to widen her stance further. "And feel what I do," he said, then pressed the bulging tip of the phallus to her. Slowly, bit by bit, he pushed it upward, the stone disappearing inside of her.

Martha's breaths came quick and her breasts and body seemed to glow as it flushed with want, her need clearly mingling with her shame.

She was lovely, Jameson had not lied. Her body was full, rounded and well used by nature, yet his touch seemed to have awakened something inside of her, something forgotten. Something newly stirred. She had more to give, much more to feel...and he took his time, showing her, showing all, that she would feel every moment of it.

He eased the thick phallus further into her, holding it still, then sliding upward again.

"Open your eyes."

Abigail lifted hers from his hand at Martha's core to Martha's eyes, now gazing at his. He stood at her side, his length pressed to her, an arm at her back as he pulled the phallus from her again, then slid it back inside, holding her as she swayed. Reminding her to open her eyes. Only a finger's width of the stone remained. "I will release it," he said softly, "You will not let it fall."

The strain on her face showed her effort to do as he said. The tension of her belly, the quivering of her legs, all signs of her wish to obey.

"Good," he said as he eased his hand away. "Feel it. Feel how it warms to your body, how it has become part of you." He took her full breast in his hand, kneaded it, all of it, gently, harshly. "What do you feel, Martha? Tell me."

"Great shame for now I crave."

He released her breast and let his hand travel over her belly to her mound where he tested the phallus. It remained inside of her, and he smiled.

"It is as it should be," he said, pressing his flattened hand to her belly. "There is no need for shame."

Martha gasped, loud and fearful. Her eyes wide. And in that moment, Abigail knew Jameson's other hand probed Martha from behind.

Abigail felt it herself. Almost ached for it. She looked down at Mercy, could she probe her without Jameson's assistance? Slowly push past the tight resistance? Would Mercy succumb to the touch or resist? Feel discomfort and shame or arousal? She cupped her oiled hand to Mercy's rump, smoothed over it, warmed it, then pressed her finger into the crease between Mercy's cheeks, brushing downward, past the puckered entry then back up to it again, Abigail's oiled finger much smaller than Jameson's...

Martha whimpered.

Abigail pressed her finger to Mercy's dark passage. Pulsed it there, unsure whether to enter.

Martha pleaded with only her eyes as she looked at Jameson.

"Feel what I do," he said, remaining at her side, watching her, not looking away, not moving. Yet Abigail knew, from the tension in Martha's body that his hand probed deeper, filling her from behind even as the phallus filled her core.

And Abigail pressed more firmly, felt resistance and stroked the tender spot, wishing to soften it as Jameson had for her. And for the others.

"Your body tenses around my fingers," he said and Martha's color deepened, rippled down her neck to her breasts, a speckled flush of want. "I feel your heat, the strength of muscle is like that of youth… " He tested the phallus again and she sighed as he pulled it from her then pushed it back in. And then his stance, rigid a moment prior, relaxed. And he smiled. "This moment is now yours," he said, "for you are unmarked."

She cried and laughed, then shook her head as if unsure, unsettled. And Abigail blinked at her own tears, recognizing the relief. The need. She withdrew her hand from Mercy, dipped her fingers into the oil once more.

"I will stop," Jameson said, "or I will continue, as you wish. You need only to speak your desire." He buried his fingers between Martha's swollen lips, his fingers rubbing her steadily. "Tell me what you seek. Release by my hand or release from it."

"Please…"

"Tell me."

"By your hand."

Though he did not tell her to look at him, she did not look away, and he held her, rubbed his fingers over her nub side to side, slowly, steadily, up and down and in circles, and Abigail reached around Mercy to touch her the same, cupping her rump with one hand, feeling her swollen nub beneath the other as Jameson felt Martha's.

"Yes," he said, "Nature is most pleased..."

With a thick deep cry, Martha trembled, her body convulsing as Jameson still rubbed her, held her. And then he stopped all movement, kept his hand on her core, his fingers still buried, not moving even as the phallus fell to the floor and all of Martha, her lips, her belly, her legs, quivered beneath his touch.

He held her until she stilled, her eyes closed, her head resting against his shoulder. And then she jolted, looked up at him. And he smiled at her, a tender smile that warmed even Abigail.

"Are you well?" he asked, slowly easing his hand from Martha's core.

"I am unsure."

"You may unclasp your hands," he said, then turned her around and settled her onto the stool. Resting his hand on her shoulder a moment before he turned from her and went to Mercy.

Abigail stood back as he pulled Mercy to standing and gripped her chin in his hand, seeming to study her face.

"Good Sir..." Abigail could not think what to say. She had not completed Mercy's examination. She had not aroused her as should be. He knew all of this.

She followed him to the chest. "She is near complete," she said, "if you will assist —"

He grabbed a wooden box from the chest. A dull thump and heavy clank of objects shifting within stirred Abigail's fears of clamps and irons and spars large and unyielding. "Good Sir...she needs but a proper touch, unlike mine, and more time..."

He went to Mercy, snatched her arm and urged her ahead of him, guiding her toward a doorway not leading to the hall. "You will slipper the feet of Martha and Hannah," he said, barely glancing at Abigail as he opened the door. "Then take them into the hall."

Abigail followed him and Mercy into another room, cold, dark, lit only by two candles set upon the far wall. "What be this place?" she asked not meaning to speak aloud.

With a long line of rope, Jameson bound Mercy's hands before her. "Rise to your toes," he said and when she did, he looped the long end of her tether over an iron ring that hung from the ceiling, pulling the rope taut until she stretched to reach it, her toes dancing upon the floor to steady herself.

"Good Sir..." What torture was this? What reason? Abigail went to him, stopped midway as he turned, his gaze hard in silent warning. She could not contain her fear or regret. "It was my touch," she said, words spilling from her. "It is lacking. I assure you, Mercy's pleasures can be roused by your hands only; you need not frighten her."

He stood before Mercy, grasped her breasts, squeezed them, tugged, forced her to stagger toward him. "Are you frightened, Mercy?" He pinched her nipples then. Milked them until they stood full and eager.

Mercy's breaths came hard. "I fear not..." her voice came deep, as though roused from her soul. "...for I am athirst."

One by one, without pause, he clamped her nipples with the same biting irons he had used on Abigail. Mercy cried out, and it was a harsh growl of a sound.

"It is only through pain when some feel pleasure." He flicked the clamps with his fingers, making them pull and pinch Mercy's nipples further. Her head lagged back, her unsteady dance unceasing. "Of this, Abigail, I assure you." He secured the clamps to a yard of leather and tethered it to an eyebolt on the wall, leaving Mercy bound by arms and nipples, staggering, unable to flatten her feet, the tether too short. Every sway, every teetering step pulling taut the clamps.

Surely pain was not Mercy's desire. Yet she did not cry in fear nor plead for release. "Good Sir, please, do not –" Abigail backed away as he stormed toward her.

He gripped her arm and pulled her into the first chamber. "Take the others into the hall." He released her, went back to the other chamber and closed the door behind him, leaving Abigail to worry over Mercy's fate.

She hurried to replace Martha and Hannah's slippers. Not speaking to them, unsure of her voice, her words, for how could she explain what happened beyond this chamber? How could she not?

Trembling, she took the others into the hall, eager for Jameson to meet them there. Hoping what he did now would rouse Mercy well and clear.

"What will happen to us now?"

Abigail turned to Hannah. Tried to smile for her. "They will see how you have been tested," she said, her voice unsteady. "And then they will dress you, as they dressed me." She turned to Martha, gripped her hand. "You will bear it without shame for your innocence has been proven. You must hold your heads high and not cover yourselves for you have naught to hide."

The creak of a door came from the opposite end of the massive hall. Abigail turned toward it and saw only blackness in that cavernous void where candlelight did not stray, the secrets there too dark to display.

Jameson came out of that darkness, his step steady. Sure.

"Good Sir…" Abigail went to him. "Mercy?"

"You will join us in the yard, Abigail." He strode past her to the others. "Then remain, for what is still to be done only I can do." He offered an arm to Hannah and Martha. Hesitantly, they each took one and walked with him to the manor doors, naked except for their slippers.

The Accused

Chapter Ten

The forest had a sound all its own. It breathed and howled and sighed.

Wind whistled mournfully around Elizabeth and night creatures scurried past her cold bare feet. The old oak moaned, perhaps lamenting her fate, while its rustling leaves shivered in the cruel night air. Her own ragged breaths mingled with it all until it echoed in her ears, muting her thoughts and her prayers.

She closed her eyes and hung her head, no longer fighting fate. The sudden snap of branches drew her attention. She listened, unseeing in the dark.

It grew louder. Like footsteps approaching. Man or beast, she did not know. She blinked into the darkness. Whoever, whatever it was, she could not fight it, could not retreat from it nor shield herself in any way.

The air changed. It grew sharp with the familiar tang of pitch. The faint glint of torchlight glowed within the trees. Drawing closer.

A smile touched her lips then faded. Giles had come back for her.

But time had been short, and it was not yet dawn. Had he come on his own or had he been sent to fetch her?

The torchlight grew brighter, and she waited, eager for Giles to reach the clearing where she might see his eyes and know his intention. He stepped beyond the brush, several paces from her. He stood tall, powerful, the torch held high, sending light and shadows dancing over his dark hood, his strong arms, and broad leather-clad chest.

Would he examine her now? Save her? Prove her innocence? She waited for him to approach, to state his purpose, for she could not see him clearly from that distance.

Confusion caught her breath as the snap of branches continued while he remained still. Two others came from the trees. They stood behind him. A man and a woman.

He approached and she kept her gaze on his, hoping to know what thoughts he had. His eyes did not comfort as before. They were hard and grave. He had not come for her; he had been sent, she was certain. That meant her fate had been determined.

She held her trembling chin high. She would neither shed tears nor plead for mercy. "You will take me to the gallows now."

He halted his stride, stood as still as the oak that held her, then slowly raised his torch higher and peered at her. "You will not speak of such things." His gruff whisper sliced the air, trembled nearly the same as hers. He looked at her a moment longer, then mounted the torch, high in its place, lighting their surroundings.

Then he turned to the others with him. "Here," he said and pointed to the ground just yards before her.

She gasped as they drew closer for in that moment she saw, laden in their arms, bundles of kindling. They placed it where Giles pointed and the meaning was plain. Cruel.

Fear tightened her chest and clawed her heart. They had chosen her fate. The governor ordered her bound but they called for her burning.

"Nay." The word broke through on her harsh breath. "I am unmarked." Could he hear her over the moans of the oak and the rustle of leaves? Would anyone hear her? Would anyone care? Or would they cheer her burning?

He drew closer and she had not the words to declare her terror. She fell silent and still, her breath held, her eyes unblinking.

He cupped a hand to her shoulder and the heat of it seared through her. It was a test, a taste of what would come next. She looked at the fire growing before her.

"The kindling is dry," he said. "It will burn quickly." He smoothed his hot hands over her spread arms. "You are chilled."

She trembled not from cold.

He glanced behind him as the others stoked the fire. "It will soon warm you."

"Warm me?"

"You are chilled."

She had thought her life over, to be ended in ashes. Relief brought sudden tears and trembling gasps she could not stop as despair ebbed and hope swelled anew within her.

"Elizabeth?" His hot hands were on her. They rubbed her arms. Held her face. "What fear is this?"

"The fire," she cried.

The gentleness was back in his eyes. "Does it not temper the chill?"

Tears of fear mingled with relief, choking her voice. "Given their will they would have me burned."

He spoke to the others. "Leave us!" Then turned back to her and set his hands on her waist.

She closed her eyes. Calmed her trembling. Welcomed the heat of his hands and the swell of the fire even as grim acceptance flamed within her, for despite his kind heart, if it were so ordered, he would surely set her within it.

"Look to me, Elizabeth."

She opened her eyes, looked beyond his black hood to his gaze; grateful tenderness still lingered there.

"It is for warmth alone."

"Why do you comfort a witch?" she asked.

"I see no witch here." He spoke so low she thought the forest had stolen his voice.

She glanced toward the others. They had reached the path, walked beyond her view. But they held no torch. How would they find their way back to town? "They believe me marked."

"Fear shows them a witch."

"Do you not have such fear?"

"Of you? Nay." He wiped the remnants of her tears. "You do not bear the mark."

She drew a fuller breath then. "Nay. I do not."

His eyes narrowed as though he smiled, and she longed to see his face beneath the hood. "It is pride which marks you, Elizabeth, not the beast."

"You have not examined me," she said. "How can you know this?"

"My hand joined the others." He smoothed one down between her breasts, searing a path along her flesh that cooled too quickly when he took it away. "You responded to our touches."

She had for she had been afraid and aroused. Shamed by touches that made her sigh and quiver for all to see. She closed her eyes against the memory.

""Twas our touches which marked you." His words and his hand, now hot on her hip, made her gasp, open her eyes.

He had said those words to the governor. Yet here she stood, bound, bare and praying night would not end. "Our dear governor would not hear of it," she said.

"You are wrong."

She trembled beneath his gaze as it fell and lingered on her breasts, thrust forward with her arms bound wide, as though she offered herself to him.

"Your neighbors would not hear of it," he said. "They would storm the manor had he not found the means with which to calm them."

Dare she hope he had banished her to the forest for safety? "Then I am to be freed?"

With the slightest glance over his shoulder to where the others had been, he drew closer to her. "They have watched you this hour," he said in a hush. "They would remain until dawn, certain familiars would find you and suckle."

It was madness. There were no familiars. No devil's teat upon her to entice them. "They would see naught but my shame as I stand bare before them for I am unmarked."

"They would see more." He dropped his hands from her. Though she sought understanding from his eyes, he avoided her gaze. "It was your wish that I might examine you." His voice pulsed beneath the snap of the fire, the moans of the oak.

"You would be thorough but kind."

Kneeling before her then, he released the ties binding her ankles. "They shall witness that which happens here."

She looked toward the thick line of trees. "They linger still?"

"Aye." He pushed her legs farther apart then pressed his large palm to a spot high on her inner thigh. A spot they said was marked. But it was not deadened as they had claimed for it burned beneath his touch. "I cannot assure your freedom," he said. "I can but seek proof enough so the others will demand it, for innocence should not be punished." He stood, looked into her eyes. "But I must know. Be this your wish?"

"It is not to you that I must submit, but to their eyes?"

"It is their eyes you must convince."

"Can you not tell them I am unmarked?"

He reached up to her bound hands and skimmed his fingertips over her palms, down the sensitive inner flesh of her arms, then down further toward her breasts. The touch so slight as to be unbearable.

She held her breath, unsure what he sought.

"Would they believe the word of a lowly watchman?" he asked as he skimmed his fingers back up to her wrists then released the ropes that held her. "Or their own eyes?"

She eased her tingling arms to her sides, her shoulders aching. And he turned her to face the oak. Soothed her shoulders, briskly rubbed her arms, then brushed her hair aside and slowly stroked a hand down her spine, gentle as though he smoothed ripples from fine cloth. The touch sent a flurry of tingles through her and she muffled a sigh of pleasure and protest.

"They would know what you feel." His breath warmed her cheek as he spoke. "They would hear it, see it." He stroked his fingers against her waist in a touch too purposeful to tickle, too light to hurt. And yet it made her tremble and ache. "They must know this be true lest they believe you have bewitched me."

Shame heat her face and she closed her eyes, wishing they would not witness the sounds and shivers caused by his touch.

"Do you not feel, Elizabeth?" His hand went to her hip and his fingers cut into her flesh as he gripped her tight, yet she made not a sound. "Has your flesh been deadened? Should I, too, feel fear?" He cupped one side of her rump, squeezed without mercy, spreading her, and at once the flames from the fire behind her were too much and not enough.

She touched her forehead to the oak. Its texture rough and unyielding, much like his hand which now stroked the tender flesh where her rump met her thigh. She shivered. No longer cold.

His strong arm wrapped around her belly and his hot body pressed to her back. "I witnessed your sighs as they examined you." His free hand slid from the back of her heated thigh to the innermost part of it, skimming the swelling flesh of her womanhood. "Fear made them blind to your desires."

She fought shameful sighs as they rose in her throat.

"They must hear it now, Elizabeth. They must see it, lest they believe this some trickery."

"Why do you do this? I am no one to you."

His fingertips brushed her mound once more, and she gasped, grasped at the bark as though it were a lover's flesh. Wanting his touch to go on. Wanting it to cease. It grew yet stronger against her nether lips, purging her of all reason as her body – cold, bare and stirred now even by the wind – was awakened, greedy for more, despite the shame of it.

"How can I know your touch is not trickery?" The breathless tone of her question belied the urgency of it.

"You cannot know." He slid a finger past her slit to touch her aching nub directly.

A cry cut through her and it was like the growl of a hungry woodland creature.

"I have seen injustice." His words rumbled within his chest as it pressed to her back. "Though none as evident as this." He withdrew his hand from her, held it before her eyes, her wetness glistening upon his fingers. "Aye or nay, Elizabeth. I must know."

She could not think. Felt weak. From the cold, from the fear. From his touch.

She had fought against this. Had refused the governor. 'Twas why she had been sent to the crowd. To submit to him would have been to dishonor herself. To submit now...

"Aye or nay?" Giles turned her to face him, and she lowered her eyes, unable to look into his. The gentle caress of fire-heated air feathered over her flesh and Giles' slow deep breaths steadied hers.

She glanced to where the others hid. Imagined their fear-filled prayers. They cared not for her virtue. It was of no importance to them. Only complete abandon would calm their fears. Only complete abandon would save her life.

She turned back to Giles, looked into his steady gaze and breathed her response. "Aye."

He smoothed his hands into her hair, combing it back from her face. "I will be thorough," he said. "I will see need rise in your eyes, I will lure it from your very core so there be no doubt." He dropped his hands and grasped her nipples between his fingers, pinching them mercilessly.

She cried out, her stunned gaze on his. "Please."

He drew closer, whispered. "You must bend to my will, Elizabeth, not I to yours. 'Tis what they must see."

He said he would be thorough. As thorough, perhaps, as those in the crowd? Or worse, for she could not resist now but submit as the others watched. Sought further signs of her guilt.

Silently, she nodded.

"On your knees," he said, pulling on her nipples, tugging her down until her knees touched the cold hard earth. Still he did not release her, but joined her, her nipples throbbing as he held them and a shameful sudden heat built within her core.

His gaze went to his hands, gripping her. "Perhaps you have been made tender by their examination," he said, "for you cry out yet my touch is not so harsh."

"It was sudden and strong."

He pinched harder, and she gasped for it was as though irons gripped her. "Shh," he said. "Do not speak but to sigh." He looked at her, his eyes expectant and she nodded.

"Good, Elizabeth." He released his hold then, and stroked a hand over her head. It was a gentle caress, too quick to soothe but tender. Rising, he looked down at her, circled her slowly. She dared not turn even as he stopped behind her and bound her wrists.

"Rise up on your knees," he said and she did.

Rustling noises came from where he stood. Leaves shuffling. Snapping of twigs. Still she did not turn but stared ahead at the flames. Hot. Crackling. Bobbing and swaying in the wind.

And then his strong legs blocked her view. She did not lift her gaze, though she ached to see his eyes and the tenderness there that seemed so far away.

He squatted before her, a long thick branch in his grasp. She stared at it, fearing his intent, thinking to call to the watchers for surely they would come to her aid should he think to harm her. The manor, the governor and all the humiliation within seemed not so cruel as Giles leaned closer to her, a hand on her knee, urging it farther from the other.

"You are mine for these moments," he said, pushing at her other knee, spreading them wide. "Your body belongs to me as the others belong to the governor." He shifted the branch, wedged it between her knees, forcing them farther apart and holding them spread until her balance teetered.

"Sit back now," he said, "and push your hips to me so I might see your arousal should it come to be."

She did as she was told, unsteady, uncomfortable and ashamed. Her body heated by the flames of the fire and strength of his gaze.

"Close your eyes," he said and she did. "Feel my touch." His hand brushed her arm and she gasped as though he stroked her core, her senses that aware. "Respond as you wish, Elizabeth, but not by word. Only by sighs or cries so they might know your responses be true."

His warm fingers traced over her breast then flicked her nipple and she did cry, her nipples sore yet eager for more.

"You crave," he said, his palm against her cheek now, his thumb stroking her lips. "Yet you resist." He parted her lips, drew his thumb over the inside of them, smearing against them until his finger felt slick and wet against her mouth. "But you will not resist for long, will you, Elizabeth…" He dribbled his hand down between her breasts to her belly, and then thrummed his wet finger against her nub and she gasped, her body heating even as he withdrew and plunged his finger back into her mouth. Her own tangy essence teased her tongue.

"If this were for my pleasure, Elizabeth, I would taste you myself." He added another finger to her mouth, and another, and she took it, sighed against it, caressing it with her tongue wanting as much to taste his flesh as hear him speak again of tasting her.

Then his fingers were gone, and her mouth was open, empty, silent until his wet fingers brushed against her nub again and she sighed, tensed, swayed. Wanting this. Hating this. Craving yet more. More came as he plunged his thick finger into her. She cried out again, her body grasping at him even as he withdrew.

And then he tapped his fingers to her, a light fluttering pressure against her nub. Her spread legs trembled as this shameful desire swirled yet higher within her.

"Please!" she cried, staring up at him, uncertain whether need should build so quickly.

His hand slapped to her mouth and she smelled her scent, sharp and bitter. His eyes, unblinking, looking into hers. "You seek release but I do not grant it." His hand was firm against her mouth. She breathed against it, inhaling her scent and his. Looking only at him and wishing away need even as her body pulsed and grasped at nothing. It yearned and yawned.

"Close your eyes," he said a second time. "And do not speak again."

She did as she was told, but as she closed her eyes, the cravings within her grew more apparent. The brush of his hand along her shoulder. Another caress down her inner thigh. Each touch light. Brief. Enough to make her tense, tip her hips further, eager to be touched, unsure whether she could withstand even the slightest brush against her.

And then all touches stopped and she knew not where he stood, where the next caress would be. There were sounds. Footsteps. Yet she felt his heat beside her. There were other sounds, other scents, as though other people stood before her now. She tried to slow her breathing. To hear past the sounds of it. She would not ask, would not peek, for she had vowed to bend to his will.

A hand cupped her breast and she screamed, a short cry. Surprised by the sudden touch. Welcoming it, aching for it to reach her nipple. Then another hand stroked her back, brushed her hair to the side. And this hand was cold. Timid. Unlike that of the watchman.

Elizabeth heard herself whimper but did not ask who dared touch her, did not draw away, nor could she – her knees spread so, herself bared to whomever stood before her, touching her, teasing her. Torture, all of it, for she detested the caresses even as she arched toward them.

She shivered, whimpered again. Unsure what to feel, what was permitted. What was expected. What might prove her innocence or guilt. She ached to ask him who stood with her, why he permitted them will over her body. And then she felt him near her.

"'Tis as before, Elizabeth." She sighed as his voice brushed her ear, soft, moist. "When you were displayed for all and aroused by their touches. Say it now, what aroused you? What shamed you, awakened you and made you yearn?" He cupped her breast, squeezed and caressed it. She knew it to be him, knew the feel of his flesh against hers. Yet she could not speak. Could not provide the response he sought, for others touched her as well, distracting her. Claiming her. Shaming her.

She shook her head, the desire to open her eyes, scream at him, run from this place, so strong her body shook, rocked, craved. "All of it," she said. "None of it. Yet I would have more..."

His hand fell to her thigh. "Look here, Mary," he said, proving Elizabeth's suspicions of others true. "The mark... it has gone."

A gasp sounded as cold hands probed the spot on her thigh where the mark had been.

"It is the devil's work!"

Elizabeth knew the voice. Recognized it, for it was the same as that of the woman who had declared her marked.

"Nay! 'Twas not the devil!" She feared punishment for speaking aloud and though she dared not open her eyes, she could not remain silent. "'Twas but the vile touches of those who examined me! Their mark lies upon my flesh, and for that I am punished..." She cried then as fear consumed her. Here, with her eyes closed, her knees forced wide, hands on her everywhere, her sex aching, she was anything but innocent. How could she ever be deemed so?

"Look to me, Elizabeth."

She opened her eyes, saw the others, the watchers, beside Giles, but turned her gaze to his. "They were forceful in their examination," he said. "'Tis why the mark was there and is now gone?"

"Aye," she said. "'Twas but a smudge or wound fashioned by their harsh and filthy hands."

Without warning and before those gathered, he pinched the spot and she cried out, shaken by the sudden pain. "See how she cries!" he said, rising. "It is not deadened as would be by the beast."

They stood back, looked at her and she could do naught but remain unsteady though proud in her innocence.

"We should fetch the governor." The young man's gaze lingered on her naked core, opened and lighted for his pleasure.

"Aye." Fear cut Mary's word close, like the snap of wood from the fire.

"Nay." Giles drew on the word. It lingered while he removed the wedge from between Elizabeth's knees and brought her to her feet. He smoothed a hand to the spot, forcing her legs to remain spread as she stood. "See it now, Mary?" He turned to look at the woman. "Is that not the mark as you saw it?"

"It has come back?" The man, along with Mary, bent low and peered at her, so close she felt the hum of their words against her flesh.

Mary knelt on the ground, her face mere inches from Elizabeth's sex. "Nay, Samuel," Mary said to the man. "'Tis a wound." Mary turned to Giles, her eyes wide, and Elizabeth took hope. "What have we done?"

"Perhaps it is right to fetch the governor," he said. "Do so. Both of you. I will tend to Elizabeth." He gripped her arm and she stumbled closer to him, pressing her thighs together as she stood.

Samuel sidled up close beside her, the coarse wool of his cloak scraping her bare flesh from shoulder to hip. "Perhaps she is marked elsewhere." His hand tangled in her hair and forced her head back. "Where do you hide the mark?" She thought to spit in his eyes but dared not as he pulled on her hair yet harder. "What form do your familiars take whence they suckle?"

"There are no familiars," she said, as fearful of him as angered, "for I have not lain with the beast."

"A witch cannot feel." Giles's palm against her hip was gentle, warm, familiar. "Yet Elizabeth felt our touches as we examined her before all." He circled her, stood behind her, cupped her breasts, caressed them, drawing Samuel's attention there. "And she felt mine," Giles said, "as I touched her before your watchful eyes."

Samuel shook his head, tightened his hold on her hair. "Perhaps her responses were feigned."

"I assure you they were not." Giles moved before her then cupped her core and thrust his fingers inside of her, making her cry out with the shock of it, the humiliation. And then he withdrew his hand and held it up toward the firelight as though some spoil from battle.

"You see, young Samuel," he said, her juices glistening upon his fingers. "Some things cannot be feigned."

"Come," Mary grabbed at Samuel's arm, already backing away. "We must tell the governor."

They turned toward the path, and Elizabeth felt her legs might crumble beneath her, so great was her relief, her hope.

As though knowing, Giles helped her to her knees and knelt before her. "We cannot know what will happen now," he said, "but I know, Elizabeth, you are not marked. I will tell them all."

She could not stop the flow of tears, her relief so great. He had sought nothing for himself, his touches for her alone, not for his own pleasure. She wished to give thanks to him. To touch him if it be his wish. "Giles..."

He brushed the tears from her face and she fell against him, her arms around his neck, her breasts pressed to the leather stretched across his chest.

"You have given me hope," she said through her tears. "While I had none before."

His arms came around her. Warm. Strong. His chest solid, his mouth so close she ached to taste it. She tipped her head toward his, wishing for a simple kiss. And then he dropped his arms from her, stood and helped her to her feet.

"The innocent have suffered enough," he said, then turned toward the fire to douse the flames.

"I am innocent."

"Aye."

She went to him. "What will happen?"

He kicked more dirt onto the dying flames. "They will see the truth," he said then faced her. "Or they will see us both hanged."

Jameson watched as the crowd cheered the dressing of Hannah and Martha. Their fear great one moment, their relief yet greater the next.

"Good Sir, please..."

He glanced at Abigail, understood her concern for Mercy but could not speak of it now. "Mary seeks my attention," he said and turned to her as she stood with the crowd.

Abigail's step was quick as she hurried beside him. "Mercy is not like the others," she said. "But she is not unfeeling. Please, you must not punish her, for it was I–"

"'Tis not everyone who fears punishment, Abigail." He reached Mary, tipped his head to her in greeting.

"Governor," she said, her eyes wide, fearful. "It is most urgent..."

The crowd's cheerful conversation grew to a loud rumble. Several women screamed and men shouted.

Jameson turned at the sounds to see Giles come from the forest with Elizabeth.

It was not dawn. She was not to be released until the sun's rise when judgment would be made. Though it was not unlike Giles to defy orders, never had he done so this boldly.

Jameson went to them, searched his friend's eyes. "What happens here?"

"Governor," Giles said with a slight bow. "As you ordered, she was bound and watched. But she is unmarked." He gripped Elizabeth's leg in his hand, spread her, displaying the mark as before. "This mark," he said to the crowd, over their rumbling, "was the result of your eager hands."

He had said those words before. Jameson knew them to be true but the people would not understand, for the devil's mark could appear and disappear, shift, tease, and confuse, as was Satan's want.

"How do you know it is not evil trickery?"

"She responded. Her body sensitive, her senses easily aroused...by the crowd and..." Giles hesitated, and Jameson feared his next words. "...and by my own touch."

The crowd's horror was loud. Raucous. Fearful. Angered.

Jameson recalled his own fear for his own soul when he had lain with Abigail then believed her marked, for a man who lies with a witch may soon host Satan himself. "You have lain with her?" he asked, afraid of the answer.

"Nay!" Elizabeth shouted. "He has not!"

"We do not know this!" Samuel Stoughton stood behind them, his birdlike face reddened from cold and self-righteousness.

"Samuel!" Mary turned on him. "'Tis a lie! You cannot deny it for we watched."

"Did he not send us ahead, Mary?" Samuel said. "Did he not lust after her? Did he not display for us proof of her arousal upon his hand?" Samuel held his own hand high and the crowd responded with shouts of horror, and their own raised fists. "What more did he do once he sent us to fetch the governor?"

The roar and crush of the crowd seemed to spur the insolent Samuel further and Jameson stood back, the time not right to stop this.

"And if it be none," Samuel shouted, "if our watchman did not seek his own fulfillment, then why? Why?" He rallied the crowd further, walked among them.

They nodded and beat the air with their fists, their torches. "It is because the witch rendered him unable! For whose pleasure is it to steal man's ability?"

"The witch!" The shout came from the crowd as though of one voice.

"Aye!" Samuel said. "For 'tis only the witch who can render a man so."

Jameson had beaten desire on many occasions. It caused great pain. Yet Giles showed no sign of discomfort. Nor a sign of contentment.

He went to Giles. Looked at him, friend to friend, though this could not be a time for friendly sympathies, for sympathies with the devil brought evil to all. There would be only one way to prove Giles unmarked. "What have you done?"

"I have proven Elizabeth unmarked."

"There is no such proof, only doubt for your soul."

Giles looked at Elizabeth. The gaze overlong and longing. Tender. Jameson understood, had felt the same for Abigail. Bewitched not by dark magic but by something more. Something pure. But he pushed those feelings aside and examined her. Fully. Proving her body untouched by the beast, her soul unmarked. Himself, safe. Giles had not been as cautious. "Giles. Do you confess here that you have lain with a witch?"

"I confess I have tested an accused and found her to be unmarked."

"Giles, please cease this madness!" Elizabeth's voice held fear. "Tell them true!"

Her stubborn pride, the cause of her pain and now Giles', had ebbed some yet still tinged her tone and posture. Naked before all, she did not cower. She was as the others, those proven unmarked by his own hand, his own eyes.

"Please!" she continued. "I saw evidence of his need, yet he did not succumb for he is not bewitched, but a gentleman."

Samuel shouted over her, "Witches defend their kind!"

"As they say." Jameson reined in his growing temper, for Samuel's fear was not as great as his bluster, yet his words would further rile the crowd.

Jameson turned to them. Their eyes were wild, their bodies huddled close, one mind shared among many. Not easily swayed or soothed. They would not find innocence, for every mark by nature would strike fear yet deeper within them.

He strode among them, let his gaze linger on each. All. "Yet what of the innocent?" he said. "Who will defend them?" He went back to Mary, declaring witchcraft one moment and innocence the next. "You?" he said to her, then turned to the old cobbler. "You, sir?" He turned again. "Or will it be you, Samuel? Can you strike guilt from your mind to see innocence with your eyes?" He stood back from them, having recaptured the attention of all. "I prove innocence should it be," he said, "as I prove guilt." He drew a full breath, called out. "And do you accept my decree?"

The crowd cheered, assuring him they still felt him fair, honest. And true.

He stepped closer to Giles. Spoke only for him. "If you continue as I fear you intend, I will be forced –"

"She is innocent."

"If that be so, you will be unmarked." Jameson glanced at Elizabeth. *Pride does not portend guilt.* They had been her words to him and he knew them to be true. But the crowd…

"My innocence will prove her innocence?"

"Aye. As will your guilt prove her guilt." He waited for something – a thought, a voice of reason from the crowd, from Giles. But reason would not come, for though they craved death to evil, they believed it lingered everywhere and the search for evil brought yet more. "Are you certain?" he said to Giles alone.

"Aye."

Sympathy and duty warred within Jameson, yet he knew of no options. "You have lain with an accused," he said for all to hear. "When a man spills his seed for a witch, he too, will bear the mark. Yet, should he not bare the mark, then she is no witch, for a servant of darkness cannot resist such evil."

He turned back to his friend, pulled the hood from his head, exposing him for all. "Speak your choice, Giles Scott," he said, saddened it could be no other way. "Will these good people determine your fate? Or will you submit to my examination?"

Giles widened his stance and clasped his hands behind his back. "It is to you that I submit."

The Accused

About the Author

Arla Dahl is a lover and avid reader of all things sexy and suspenseful. In her Immoral Virtue Trilogy, the horrors of the 17th Century witch trials are exposed, examined and reversed. Deeply moved by the viciousness of times, Arla created stories that would turn history on its ear and make that which labeled the accused susceptible to the temptations of evil, into the one thing that would set them free. Lust.

Stay engaged!

Find Arla online

Facebook at www.facebook.com/arladahl

Twitter: https://twitter.com/ArlaDahlAuthor

Her blog: http://www.arladahl.com/notes/

See also, her website

www.arladahl.com

The Accused

Arla Dahl

Immoral Virtue Series
Book Three

The Watchman

For when those in authority neglect to reprove sin,
then very often the good are punished
with the wicked
-Heinrick Kramer, 1486

EXCERPT
The Watchman (Immoral Virtue, #3)

Giles stood rigid before Jameson. Neither resisting nor cowering. He would bear the humiliation of the crowd's taunts and touches. And Jameson would permit it, require it for Giles as he had for the women who endured the same shame this night. Yet the vigor with which the crowd sought to examine him proved their judgment clouded, their minds believing only evil surrounded them, and he would not subject his friend to that.

Jameson glanced up at the sky. Too soon dawn would be upon them, bringing with it final judgment of the accused.

He turned toward the manor, taking Giles with him. "You will follow," he said to Elizabeth, hating the sight of her at that moment, for it was her pride, her resistance, her foolery, which had led his friend to this fate.

She took a step toward him as Samuel Stoughton burst from the crowd, his skinny pale fingers closing over Elizabeth's upper arm once he reached her.

"She should be bound," he said in that hawkish barking way of his. "She should be spread before us all lest the mark fade and reappear from her flesh once again."

A rumble came from the crowd as the villagers debated Samuel's wisdom. Some eager to see Elizabeth opened to their eyes again, some too frightened by the evil they believed lay deep within her heart.

Samuel tugged her back toward the platform where she had been spread and bound just an hour prior. Where every inch of her flesh had been examined.

Where every crease and fold and orifice was tested for sensitivity by the crowd until they discovered the mark upon her thigh.

Fear such as Jameson had not seen in Elizabeth's eyes this night shone bright, wild and pleading. The extent of the crowd's cruelty no doubt still clear in her mind. She deserved punishment, but none such as this.

He turned from her, spoke to the crowd's fears. "You would have a witch bound before you, Samuel? A witch who would render you—as all men—either incapable or so lustful he cannot control himself, even if pigs or dogs be his only sheath?"

Shrieks of shock, and shouts of rage, came from the crowd as was Jameson's desire.

Samuel dragged Elizabeth closer to the platform, the shackles hanging from the beam that topped it clanking harshly with every blast of blistery air.

Elizabeth stumbled behind Samuel. Her frightened eyes darting from one in the crowd to another. Her red hair, wild in the cold wind. Her naked flesh pale and spotty in the frigid night. And yet she did not resist. The fire in her heart doused... but why? She had refused to submit to Jameson earlier, when he could have spared her this shame. When he could have sought to prove her innocence, taken his time with her examination, touched her gently, not crudely as was the habit of this mob. He would have awakened her desires, forced her to feel his touches and to respond, for it is only the witch who cannot feel. And he would have been sure to see she felt his every touch. His every caress. His every probe.

"This witch will have no power over us," Samuel shouted as the crowd parted to let him pass. "Pious men cannot be harmed by the likes of her."

Jameson remained in place, unwilling to chase after Samuel. "'Tis the pious Satan most wishes to turn," he said calmly but firmly so all would hear. "And 'tis Satan's pleasure that witches fulfill." He settled his gaze on Samuel's, daring the insolent fool to challenge him further, not speaking again until the moment Samuel drew his own breath for words. "Tell me, Samuel," Jameson said, "is it not Satan's desire to fill our hearts with lust?"

"Aye. 'Tis so."

"Then it would please him, would it not, to see men rendered incapable so they might leave their women yearning?" He did not wait for Samuel's response. "It would. For who better to seduce needy women than the greatest seducer of all?"

He let the crowd's nervous grumbling linger, then strode forward and snatched Elizabeth from Samuel's grasp.

"Nay." Jameson turned with her toward the manor. "All would be safer with her locked inside where I might keep close watch."

She hurried beside him, not struggling even in his grasp whereas before, a mere glance from him sent her pride soaring, her venomous words of resistance sealing her fate. They reached Giles and Jameson nudged him until Giles led the way up the manor steps.

Inside, Jameson flung Elizabeth from his grasp. She stumbled against the wall, and he pressed his hand to her neck, holding her there, pushing her further back to that wall, resenting her for adding to the pain and chaos of this night.

"Your stubborn pride is to blame for what happens here now," he said.

*Though he would resist
the touch of another man's
hands, it is only the witch
who cannot feel.*

Winter 2015
Immoral Virtue Trilogy: Book Three

The Watchman